Wh

Rufus silently a
not for the first time since climbing into
Rachel's vehicle back at the Civic Center.

It wasn't as if she'd put a gun to his head
and forced him to join her. But something
about this woman played havoc with his
usual self-restraint. People thought he was
shy when in truth he simply didn't want
to connect with anyone. And he was damn
good at avoidance.

Until today. Until *her.*

Dear Reader,

One of my favorite fairy tales is *Beauty and the Beast*. I love that Belle is able to sense something redemptive beneath the brutish exterior of the beast long before the outer world sees his human side. And the transformation that takes place once the beast feels worthy of her love never fails to make my heart swell with hope and joy.

Rufus, the hero of this book, hides his true self beneath layers of flannel and a gruff demeanor meant to keep people at bay. There's a reason Rachel Grey calls him "Big Foot's second cousin." But when Rachel slams the door on her old life and heads to Sentinel Pass in the Black Hills, she isn't looking for a gorgeous heartthrob to sweep her off her feet. Her handsome ex-husband taught her that superficial beauty is only useful as a marketing tool, without honor and depth of character to flesh it out. And almost as if to prove her point, she falls for Rufus, hermit and solitary rustic artist.

Rachel and Rufus's story is the first of four more SPOTLIGHT ON SENTINEL PASS books. Look for old friends and new faces in upcoming stories. The members of the Wine, Women and Words book club continue to meet regularly and welcome new members, like Rachel, into their midst. Please check out the updated list of titles at www.debrasalonen.com.

Happy reading,

Debra Salonen

Until He Met Rachel
Debra Salonen

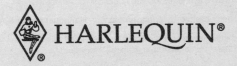

TORONTO • NEW YORK • LONDON
AMSTERDAM • PARIS • SYDNEY • HAMBURG
STOCKHOLM • ATHENS • TOKYO • MILAN • MADRID
PRAGUE • WARSAW • BUDAPEST • AUCKLAND

Recycling programs
for this product may
not exist in your area.

ISBN-13: 978-0-373-71633-3

UNTIL HE MET RACHEL

Printed in U.S.A.

ABOUT THE AUTHOR

Debra Salonen was awarded her silver anniversary pin from Harlequin in July 2009, celebrating the release of her 25th book. Although her sister's health crisis prevented Debra from attending the awards ceremony in Washington, D.C., Deb celebrated the occasion with the help of her sister, Jan, and members of her local Wine, Women and Words book club shortly before Jan passed away. The memory is one Deb will treasure always.

Books by Debra Salonen

HARLEQUIN SUPERROMANCE
1196—A COWBOY SUMMER
1238—CALEB'S CHRISTMAS WISH
1279—HIS REAL FATHER
1386—A BABY ON THE WAY
1392—WHO NEEDS CUPID?
      "The Max Factor"
1434—LOVE, BY GEORGE
1452—BETTING ON SANTA
1492—BABY BY CONTRACT*
1516—HIS BROTHER'S SECRET*
1540—DADDY BY SURPRISE*
1564—PICTURE-PERFECT MOM*
1588—FINDING THEIR SON*

*Spotlight on Sentinel Pass

SIGNATURE SELECT SAGA
BETTING ON GRACE

HARLEQUIN AMERICAN ROMANCE
1114—ONE DADDY TOO MANY
1126—BRINGING BABY HOME
1139—THE QUIET CHILD

For Jan O'Brien, my sister and best friend, who passed away at age 72, after a brief but valiant fight with lung cancer. Her unfailing support, dedicated proofreading and love of books helped me to become the writer I am.

CHAPTER ONE

"SELL THE PORSCHE."

Rachel Grey clutched her chest theatrically. "Mother, I'd sell you into white slavery before I'd sell the Porsche. It's the only thing I'm taking away from my marriage. A marriage you pushed for, I might add."

"The fact that you and Trevor never found the common ground necessary to make your marriage a success is not my fault," her mother stated imperiously. A recently retired bank V.P., Rosaline Treadwell was a master at passing the buck. "The car is completely impractical."

"That's what I like best about it." Rachel crossed her arms in a way her mother would recognize from the many childish rebellions Rachel had fought—and lost—over the years. She wasn't losing this one—childish or not.

"Forty thousand dollars could provide you with enough of a cushion that you could stay in Denver and find a real job. You wouldn't be reduced to working as a clerk in a tourist trap." Her mom made a sweeping, all-encompassing gesture that would have caused Rachel to die of embarrassment if the establishment's owner, Char Jones, had been present.

"Native Arts isn't a tourist trap. It's more of an art

gallery than a store. The local artists are amazing and I love working here. The energy is…electrifying."

Rosaline would never be so crass as to roll her eyes in public, but Rachel could tell her mother had no interest in, or respect for the creative process. She'd never forget an argument they'd had her senior year of high school.

"I've been accepted at a design school on the West Coast, Mom. Isn't that great?"

"Not if you plan to pay for it using the money I put into your college fund. Accounting might not be as glamorous as advertising, but it's a lot more predictable. Death and taxes are never going out of style."

That had been the beginning of a month-long battle. In the end, Rachel had opted to stay in Denver, live at home and graduate from business school with an emphasis on accounting and statistics. The chief lesson Rachel learned from this was the person whose hand controlled the purse strings had the most pull. Too bad the same was true about love. The person who pulled the most strings controlled the pocketbook—broken marriage vows or no broken marriage vows.

"The nature of this business isn't the point, is it?" Rachel asked, shifting impatiently from one well-broken-in UGG boot to the other. "Even retail might be acceptable if the high-end designer boutique were back home, right? Please don't take this the wrong way, Mother, but I'm moving to the Black Hills to get away from Denver."

"Away from me, you mean."

Rachel heaved a sigh and shook her head. "I knew you'd take it the wrong way. Mom, I need a fresh start, a clean break. Why can't you see that and support my decision—even if it's the wrong decision? Just this once."

Her mother's carefully painted lips pressed together in a way Rachel knew all too well. Rosaline Treadwell would have made a fabulous wartime general. "Never lose sight of your goal," she'd admonished so often in Rachel's childhood, Rachel had threatened to have it engraved on her mother's tombstone. What Rosaline couldn't understand was she and her daughter had different ideas about what constituted a goal.

Mom held up one perfectly manicured hand and listed her complaints, finger by finger. "My daughter is moving to a new state with no job, no real home and only a vague idea of what she wants to do with her life. And I'm supposed to be happy about that?"

"And a forty-thousand-dollar sports car," Rachel added.

Her mother's eyes narrowed. "In the dead of winter," her mother finished, waving her pinkie for emphasis. "I honestly don't understand you, Rachel. Are you certain you don't want to *try* therapy?"

That subject had been covered at length in a recent e-mail that had included links to several outpatient clinics in the greater Denver area and one in Taos, New Mexico—so no one from the bank would hear about her daughter's collapse, Rachel assumed.

Rachel didn't bother trying to repress her sigh. "I'll make you a deal, Mom. If Sentinel Pass doesn't work out—if I'm flat broke and miserable a year from now—I'll move home and see any doctor you want. Okay?"

There was a pause of a heartbeat or two before her mom said, "Are you absolutely certain you're not here to try to meet a man? Maybe an actor from that silly TV show, *Sentinel Passtime?* My friends are concerned that you've become addicted to the glamorous lifestyle you had with Trevor and can't give it up."

Rachel's shudder came from deep inside. "Are those the same friends who pushed you to introduce me and Trevor in the first place? I promise you I'm done with pretty-boy prima donnas." She paused. "Wait. Can a man be a prima donna? Wouldn't that make him a prima Donald?"

Her mother's slow, dramatic inhale made Rachel rush to get back on topic. "Mom, I married superficial charm once in my life, and once was enough. If I ever fall in love again, it's going to be with a plain, down-to-earth, what-you-see-is-what-you-get kind of man. Homely, hook-nose, bald, whatever. Looks only count in advertising. I learned that the hard way."

Her mother didn't seem convinced, but she set aside the topic of love and returned to the one of location. "Please explain why you chose this town, Rachel. A small, flash-in-the-pan overnight sensation. I know you and your brother are close, and I will admit that Kat has grown on me. I understand your wanting to help plan their wedding, but surely you can do that from Denver."

I could, but that's not the point. "Mom, face it. There's nothing for me in Denver. The big, beautiful house that Trevor was so quick to get listed on the celebrity home tour is as good as sold. Thanks to the crazy economy, my dependable accounting job is history. Last hired, first fired." A job her mother got for her and Rachel had never really liked, although she had, toward the end of her employment, found ways to make it her own. "I like this place."

Rosaline didn't reply.

"I like the people. I love my future sister-in-law and her sons. I can't wait to be part of the Wine, Women and Words book club. Char is a gas. We bonded when she came back from her trip to California, and I feel as though we have a true friendship blossoming. I need that."

"Fine. Do what you want. You always have."

It took every bit of self-control Rachel possessed not to scream, "What are you talking about? I usually do what *you* want. And always have."

True, mother and daughter had butted heads most of Rachel's life. But in the end, her intelligent, opinionated and strong-willed mother almost always got her way—Rachel's father had insisted on it when he was alive.

Rachel wasn't sure what was fueling her current rebellion. Maybe Jack's unexpected too-early-for-midlife crisis was the catalyst. Her straight-arrow, look-before-you-leap brother shocked everyone when he bought a motorcycle, rode to the Black Hills and fell in love with Kat, a single mom with two sons.

Rachel felt a little sheepish trailing after her big brother this way, but Jack knew about her secret dream to open her own Web design and online marketing company. Probably a foolish plan given the fact she lacked any real training or experience, but she'd dabbled in Web design for years. In fact, the mock-up she'd done for Trevor the day after they met at her mother's big charity golf event had impressed him so much he'd asked her out. He claimed to have been blown away by her innate ability to grasp the inner Trevor Grey. The man behind the public persona.

She'd been flattered. He'd played to her ego and swept her off her feet. When he asked her to marry him, her instincts told her to slow down and see how they gelled over time. But her mother had berated Rachel's cold feet. "Only a fool would pass up a fine catch like Trevor Grey," Mom had said.

So, Rachel ignored her misgivings and let herself become swept away by the energy and craziness of planning her own wedding. Afterward, her mother walked around for weeks with a copy of *InStyle*'s Celebrity Bridal edition to show her friends.

Unfortunately, Trevor wasn't good at math. He didn't understand that one plus one was supposed to equal two, not three or four or as many meaningless trysts as he wanted. Besides feeling angry and humiliated, Rachel slowly came to realize her self-confidence had suffered the biggest blow. She'd failed to trust her instincts. What if she made the same mistake again?

That mistrust was one reason she was moving away from Denver. Away from her mother. Mom had made it clear a long time ago how much stock she put in creative endeavors. The less she knew about Rachel's current plans, the better. At the moment, Rachel and Jack had agreed to let Mom believe that she was here temporarily to plan his wedding and do some fill-in jobs until Jack's new dental office was up and running.

"I need to start setting out the Christmas displays for Char," she said, gesturing toward a stack of boxes. "And you don't want to get caught in traffic when you reach Denver, right? Drive carefully and call me when you get home, okay?"

Rachel could tell there was a lot more that her mother wanted to say, but Rosaline managed to contain herself by pressing her lips together for several seconds before she gave Rachel a quick, perfunctory hug then walked away.

Rosaline paused at the door of her Cadillac Seville but didn't wave at Rachel. Instead, she scowled at Rachel's small, midnight blue payoff for a quick, quiet divorce.

Her mother was right, of course. They both knew it. Rachel would have been smart to sell the car months ago, before the economy took a downward spiral. But as long as she was driving the Porsche she could pretend that she'd come out of her marriage ahead. That her spirit was strong and vital like the perfectly tuned engine under the sleek, sexy hood. That she wasn't damaged goods, someone to be pitied. Or worse, such a lousy wife she couldn't keep a husband.

If Rachel were a bigger person, she would have admitted that she'd listed the car online last week and had several very promising responses, including one from a guy in Denver. She planned to meet him next week when she returned home to finish packing her stuff. A trip her mother knew nothing about.

Rachel felt an uncomfortable pressure on her chest as she watched the Caddie pull out of the gravel parking lot onto the highway. *Bad daughter,* she silently castigated. But she had her reasons for keeping mum on both subjects.

For one, if her mother knew exactly how precarious Rachel's finances were, Rosaline would have felt compelled to offer Rachel a loan. Or worse, an advance on her inheritance. Either way, the money would have been one more blow to Rachel's pride.

Secondly, Rachel didn't want her plans to interfere with Rosaline's golf getaway to Florida. With any luck, Mom would be so charmed by the weather, she'd become a snowbird like several of her friends. Which probably sounded like a terrible thing for a daughter to think, but, at the moment, distance sounded like the best way to keep her mother out of her business.

Was she crazy to risk everything on an unproven business in a remote corner of the world? Mom would certainly say so. But Rachel knew that the Internet didn't care where you lived, if you were good at your job. But was she? That remained to be seen.

She could crunch numbers with the best of them, but could she blend that left-brain functionality with her right hemisphere's love of art, color and composition?

She fished a bright, glossy business card out of the front pocket of her jeans. WebHead—Designed to Sell, Rachel Treadwell Grey, owner. She would have given one to her mother if she thought for a moment that Mom would have been happy for her.

Despite their differences, Rachel loved her mother, and wishing things were different between them was a waste of effort. She set her card on the counter, intending to leave it by the register for Char after she finished unpacking the dozen or so boxes.

She grabbed the retractable box cutter and was poised to slice into the largest of the designated boxes when her cell phone started playing "Red, Red Wine"—the ring tone she'd given Char.

"Hi. How's Spearfish?"

Char had gone to the northern Hills town to register for classes at Black Hills State College. "It would be better if I'd called first—as you suggested. The registrar's office is closed for Thanksgiving break, for heaven's sake. What's wrong with me?"

Rachel smiled. "You're in love. And you're excited about starting a new phase of your life. I understand completely since I'm doing the same thing." She coughed. "Well, not the going-back-to-college or falling-in-love parts, but…" She let out a small howl of frustration. "You know what I mean."

Char's laugh was inclusive, not mean-spirited. "I do. I truly do. And, trust me, Sentinel Pass is the perfect place to reinvent yourself. Worked for me."

That was true. Char Jones had started with very little, built a business, created a diverse network of friends and reconnected with the love of her life—and the son she'd given up for adoption. And, thanks to Rachel's tweaking of the Native Arts' Web site, Char's online sales had doubled from this time last year. A fact that encouraged Rachel to believe she was on the right track, career-wise.

"So, are you coming straight back?"

"No. I drove to Sturgis to see Damien and Eli. It's such a nice, clear day we've decided to hike to the top of Bear Butte for a picnic."

Rachel leaned sideways to look out the large picture window at the front of the store. A small amount of snow remained in piles near the edge of the highway, but the bright winter sun seemed to hold a special sparkle. "Cool," she said. "Some might say chilly."

"Some already have," Char returned, a laugh in her voice. "Damien is such a California kid. His blood hasn't had time to acclimate, but Eli bought him some new boots and heavy wool socks. He'll be fine."

Spoken like a true mother. A supportive, your-kid-can-do-no-wrong kind of mother.

They talked a few minutes longer about the holiday

displays before Char said, "I hear the pounding of size eleven footsteps. Do whatever you want, Rae. I trust you. You have a real gift for display. Go for it."

Rachel's throat squeezed tight. "Thanks. I—"

"Gotta run. See you later this afternoon."

Rachel snapped her phone closed. She allowed herself a brief moment to savor Char's praise then she pocketed the phone and got to work. It was one thing to claim you had an eye for design but quite another to actually make the idea in your mind come to life in the space and time allotted.

The Internet was her medium of choice, but she believed in the power of word of mouth. If she did a fantastic and original job on these displays for Char, word would get around. It might be nice to snag a celebrity or two as her mother had suggested, but the person she most wanted to work for was a reclusive, natural mediums artist named Rufus Miller.

Jack's fiancée, Kat Petroski, had one of Miller's rustic birdhouses on her deck. Made entirely of scraps of wood, moss, bark, pebbles and other objects found in nature, the compact, whimsical piece spoke to Rachel in a way she didn't quite understand. She had yet to meet the man behind the birdhouses, but she definitely wanted him as a client. If what Kat said was true, Rufus's birdhouses were the mere tip of the iceberg where his talent was concerned.

All she had to do was angle an invitation to meet the shy recluse. Oh…and buy a four-wheel-drive vehicle to get up the mountain to reach his remote cabin. His one-of-a-kind art wouldn't make either of them rich, but she didn't care. Rich wasn't everything it was cracked up to be—not when it came with a huge emotional price tag.

After opening the flaps of the first box, she dug through a sea of packing peanuts to withdraw a five-inch banana-shaped hunk of newsprint. She unwrapped the figurine with care.

"Oh," she exclaimed, palming the raku-fired ceramic Wise Man. "Nice."

She let the packaging material drop to the floor as she examined the piece. Dark, earthy colors with a copper hue that added a hint of the exotic. She set it on the glass shelf to her right then eagerly dug into the box to find the rest of the crèche. Each figure was another masterpiece.

She was so engrossed in her mission of discovery she nearly missed the ding-dong sound announcing the arrival of a customer. "I'll be right with you," she hollered.

Muttering under her breath, she glanced at the grouping of holy figurines and shook her head. "Mary? Joseph? Where's your baby?"

Bending over, she pawed elbow-deep through the box until her fingers closed around something small and solid. "Ah-ha," she cried. "I found Him."

She straightened, lifting her arm overhead triumphantly. Her hold on the holy infant faltered the instant she realized her customer was a towering monolith of a man with a bushy mop of a beard that seemed to start an inch or so below his fiercely black eyes. His wild, unruly hair—a color of brown dark enough to be called black—seemed to possess a life of its own, except in the places where his hat had tamed it. A fleece-lined red plaid hat with earflaps that he held crushed to the chest of his hazardous-waste-material orange plaid jacket. His leather gloves were probably fourteen sizes larger than the pair in her purse.

Rachel lowered her hand until it was level with her face. "I found Jesus."

A man who could pass for Bigfoot in plaid might be common in Sentinel Pass, but the city-girl part of her brain was releasing boatloads of adrenaline along with the sage advice: run. Her toes gripped the insides of her boots. Her knees quivered. But her legs didn't move. Not even when the colorful giant threw back his head and started to laugh.

A name flashed into her head. Rufus Miller. She didn't know why. No one had described him as lumbering and hirsute.

No...it couldn't be. Her white-knuckle grip on the beatifically smiling infant lessened. "Um...uh...hi. My name is Rachel Grey. You wouldn't by any chance be Rufus Miller, would you?"

It took Rufus a minute to get his laughter under control. He didn't have cause to laugh very often, but the expression on this pretty young woman's face— part triumph, part terror—seemed a very fitting culmination of the changes that had taken place in his world over the past few months. His days of peaceful obscurity were over. He needed to make a living again.

Again being the operative word. He'd socked away plenty of money at the time of his premature retirement. Unfortunately, the economy of the world-at-large, and a certain infamous greedy investment counselor, had changed things. He and his dogs wouldn't starve anytime soon, but he couldn't keep funding the cause nearest and dearest to his heart if he didn't start bringing in some cash. Sooner, rather than later.

He ignored the woman's question. He'd seen that

"Hey, I recognize you" look a thousand times if not more. "Aren't you the model from the Calvin Klein ad?" they'd ask, touching his arm, his lapel, even his derriere, as if seeing his bare skin in print gave them some kind of ownership.

"Is Char here?" He didn't know the owner of Native Arts well, but her distinctive hair color, which seemed to change on a whim, made her pretty hard to miss. He appreciated individualism. The woman in front of him was a bit too chic—despite the scruffy boots—to qualify as different. What did she say her name was? Rachel Grey? Why did that sound familiar?

"No. Char's gone today. I'm working for her. Crafting some holiday displays." She waggled the ceramic piece she'd been holding like an atomizer of Mace.

Rufus glanced around. She'd either just started or she was really bad at her job.

As if hearing his critique, she quickly disposed of the small figurine and stepped around the debris. She held out her hand. "You are Rufus, aren't you? I e-mailed you, but Char said you're somewhat hit-and-miss with the Internet. I was hoping to talk to you about revamping your online presence. To up your sales."

It took him a moment to get his head—his ego—back in the present. This wasn't about R. J. Milne, semi-naked underwear model. The man he'd been, in another life. This was about his current persona. Rufus Miller, backwoods loner-turned-businessman.

"Um…"

"Your preholiday sales," she added. "Something we'd have to jump on right away so you can get the most bang for your buck." She cringed and quickly apologized. "Forgive the cliché, but I didn't have time to think about my presentation beyond the rough draft stage. Of course, I could and will give you a more complete analysis of your marketing needs after we've talked."

His palms started to sweat and his throat shunk to a pinhole. What she was suggesting had already crossed his mind. In fact, he'd decided only that morning to invest in a Web site and try to take his sales to the next level.

In theory.

He'd known that would mean inviting the outside world back into his life. He simply hadn't expected the outside world to arrive as a tsunami surfed by a beautiful stranger. A woman who... "Wait. Your name is Rachel?"

She blinked her long, pretty eyelashes. "Yes."

"Kat's Rachel?"

Her smile showed her relief. "Yes. Kat is marrying my brother, Jack. You're coming to the wedding, aren't you? I saw your name on the guest list. I could have waited to approach you then with my sales pitch, but since the wedding is four days after Christmas, I figured that wouldn't do either of us any good, would it?"

He shook his head, aware of her quick survey. He gave her credit for not appearing too repelled. He'd cultivated this disguise for a reason—it kept people at arm's length. It didn't seem to work with her.

"You are coming, right? I don't remember seeing your RSVP."

He liked Kat. She'd been the first to see the potential in his hobby and had encouraged him to sell his birdhouses on craigslist and eBay. She was the perfect kind of friend for someone like him—too busy with her own life to be all that interested in his. But he had no intention of attending a wedding. God, no.

"Kat told me a while ago that Char might sell some of my birdhouses. On consignment."

She used the side of her finger to rub the tip of her nose. A stalling tactic, he realized. "I'm sure she would and I would be happy to give her cell phone a try, but she said something about hiking Bear Butte. I don't know if she'll have reception there. Would you like to wait?"

Damn. The physical drive into town wasn't that big a deal, but getting past the mental hurdle he'd slowly acquired from his self-imposed isolation was more taxing. "No. I have to get back to work."

"Oh. Sure. Great work ethic. That's good to know. Did you bring any of your birdhouses with you? I would be happy to take care of them until you can connect with Char."

He had a truck full of his latest creations, but he had no intention of handing them over to a stranger. Especially a stranger who wanted something from him. His social instincts were rusty, but he sensed she had some kind of agenda that went beyond wanting to pitch a marketing plan. "I'll leave one. If she wants more, I'll check back next week."

He could tell that idea didn't set well with Rachel. Her lips, as shapely and shiny as those of any model he'd ever worked with, pressed together primly. The gesture reminded him of his mother, although Mom had hardly ever scolded him or his brother. Mom had been the easygoing type, happy and very tough to rile up—until the accident. "Happy" hadn't been part of their family dynamic after that.

"May I see them?"

The cramped feeling in his belly increased. Selling anonymously over the Internet was one thing. Having his questionable attempt at art critiqued, *mano-a-mano*, was quite another. But what choice did he have?

None.

"They're in my truck."

She quickly tidied her work area so the box wasn't blocking the aisle and the fragile ceramic pieces were out of harm's way then turned to follow him.

"It's cold. Don't you want a coat?"

She made a scoffing sound. "I won't freeze."

He didn't argue. He got the feeling she did what she wanted despite what anyone else thought. He admired that in a person. Independence was his one claim to fame. Or had been at one time in his life.

His dogs, all smushed together on the passenger seat of his truck, greeted him as if he'd been gone several days, not minutes. Three vociferous mutts he'd slowly acquired over the years. Only Chumley, the nine-year-old arthritic black Lab, had been an intentional acquisition. Fred and Rat-Girl had joined his canine family by accident and circumstance, respectively.

"Hush."

Fred—the half pit, half who-knew-what?—let out a whimper clearly audible through the glass. Fred hated to be scolded. Not surprising, really. The poor animal had shown up two years earlier, limping from what looked like shotgun pellets in his rump. His name had been embroidered on the corner of the tattered scarf tied around his neck. Someone had loved him once, but that someone had let him go—or tried to kill him. Rufus never bothered to look for his previous owner.

Rat—the only female of the bunch—had arrived in the middle of the night last summer during a torrential downpour. Shivering and exhausted, she'd literally dropped at his feet, her longish golden red coat plastered to her bulging sides like a drowned rat. She'd given birth an hour later to three tiny souls, all not breathing. Rufus's heart had ached watching her lick each one clean and gently nuzzle them, trying to coax them to life. He and the other two dogs had buried the little bodies the next morning up on the ridge above his house.

Oddly, that was where he'd found the inspiration behind his newest rendition of his hobby. A part-time pastime he was hoping to turn into a paying enterprise.

He didn't know how or why the idea entered his mind, but once he started puttering with the twigs and moss and bark and weathered branches he'd discovered around the burial site, his imagination had shifted to high gear and he'd found himself remembering a time in his life when art had had meaning and importance. Seventh grade. The last time he let himself tap in to that talent.

"These are different," he warned her, opening the tailgate of his vintage diesel truck. He liked its beat-up, rusted exterior, but beneath the hood was a perfectly tuned engine. His mechanic in Sturgis made sure of it. "Kat and her friend Jenna called my first ones *suggestive.* Never saw it myself, but I quit makin' them. Didn't like the e-mails I was getting." He crammed his hat on his head, letting the flaps hang loose by his jaw.

There were twisted people in the world. He knew. He'd been one. And he wanted no part of that now.

"I call these Dreamhouses."

He reached for the closest one. A two-story model. "Every bit of it except the nails and glue comes from the woods around my place," he told her. "See the chimney? I left it open so you can write notes, fold up the paper and drop it into a sealed compartment on the inside. Whatever you write is a secret. Just between you and your god, or…whatever."

He felt embarrassed and slightly out of breath. He never talked that much at one time.

"Great name. I can do a lot with that, marketing-wise. May I?" She held out her hands to accept it. He recognized an intensity in her face that went beyond appreciating his work. She turned it, slowly taking in the detail. He was proud of these latest pieces, but nervous, too.

"This is amazing, Rufus. May I call you that?" She barely glanced his way to see his nod. "I absolutely love it. I'd buy it in a heartbeat, if I had a porch of my own." She lowered the Dreamhouse to look at him.

"Let me lay my cards on the table, as they say. At the moment, I'm homeless and between jobs." She flashed him a smile that seemed turned inward. "I was a corporate bean counter in Denver for the past six years, but as you might imagine, there's not as much money around to count these days," she said lightly. "So, my brother is helping me move. I'll be staying in Libby McGannon's guest house until I can find a more permanent place. If everything works out. Career-wise."

He didn't ask for more details. He knew the McGannon place. Everyone in town did. He'd been sorry to hear about the grandmother's recent passing. Libby was a kind and friendly woman he'd communi-

cated with at the post office on the rare occasion when
he needed stamps.

"So…you want I should leave…a couple of 'em?"
He sometimes forgot to speak in a stumbling, back-
woodsy manner, but he tried.

"No," she exclaimed, lifting the tarp to see more. "I
want them all."

She was moving fast—either the cold was getting to
her or she was excited about his work. He didn't have
enough faith in his art to automatically assume the latter.

"These are wonderful, Rufus. Your style is rich,
unique and mystical," she said, her tone almost embar-
rassingly enthusiastic. Her words sounded fake but she
seemed real. He wasn't sure what to believe.

"Here's what I'd like to do," she said, turning to face
him. "With your permission, I'll photograph them and
work up a couple of design prototypes. Naturally, we'll
also display them here in Char's shop. Every sale
counts, right? But I think you'll be surprised by how
much demand there will be once we get these into the
online market."

"Even in the bad economy?"

"Because of the bad economy," she said, stressing the
first word. "People need to foster hope in their dreams
more than ever. I sincerely hope I can do your work
justice and you'll consider becoming my first client."

The word jolted him. He'd been a client before. His
agent had made a boatload of money from R. J. Milne.
His financial advisor had made even more—not legiti-
mately, of course, but still. Was he ready to be a client
again? He'd have to think about it.

"I'll leave two. Where do you want 'em?"

He saw the momentary dimming of the excitement in her eyes, but he didn't let it bother him. He'd learned the hard way he couldn't be responsible for making other people happy. To paraphrase a popular bumper sticker: Disappointment happens.

"Right inside the door, please. I think I'll create a Christmas village look around them in the front window. How much are you asking for them?"

He swallowed harshly. He'd debated that question all the way down the hill. He took a chance and went high.

Her beautifully shaped eyebrows raked together. "Oh, no. Much too low. Let's try them at twice that plus Char's commission. If they don't get snapped up in a couple of days, I'll knock them down to a sale price."

He doubted they'd sell as fast as she imagined, but he couldn't fault her enthusiasm. She had an air about her that reminded him of the view from the top of his ridge after a storm. Electric and filled with promise and potential.

Business potential, he reminded himself sternly. That was what he needed in his life. That was all he needed.

CHAPTER TWO

SEX TOYS.

Rachel paused, one hand on the drawer pull. She hadn't opened the bottom drawer of her bedside nightstand since her divorce, but she could picture what was in there.

To pack or not to pack? That was the question that would have had her mother rolling over in her grave…if her mother were dead. Which she wasn't. Yet.

Their argument two days earlier in Sentinel Pass had created a new strain on their already challenging relationship. Rachel understood her mother's concern, and she could appreciate how unnerving it might be to lose both of your children to another state. But at this point in Rachel's life, it was either move or commit matricide.

She opened the drawer enough to peek. Naughty, silly, funny shower gifts. The more over-the-top the better. Most were still in their original packaging. Trevor hadn't been the sexually adventurous type. Rachel had hoped that would eventually change, but they hadn't had time.

A clutching sensation that usually meant tears started in her throat and began to migrate upward, but she refused to give in to it. Yes, she missed being married. Not the lies, the passive-aggressive manipulation or the drama that had surrounded their divorce. But she missed the sex—and the physical closeness of two bodies sharing the same bed, kissing good-morning, a stray hug or two during the day.

Too bad we weren't close emotionally. Impatient with herself for wallowing even momentarily in If-Only-Ville, she swallowed the lump in her throat and yanked open the drawer. She'd dump the entire thing in a box and worry about disposing of the contents later. Who knew when she might meet someone she liked enough to risk getting involved? If there was a shelf-life date on any of these things, she'd add them to the stuff going to Goodwill.

She had her hand on a package of French ticklers when a voice asked, "When are they coming?"

She spun around so fast, she nearly slid off the bare pillow-top mattress. "What? Who?"

"The movers," Jack said, his tone implying she was a little slow.

Rachel used her foot to close the drawer. "Tomorrow afternoon. Why?"

He patted the cell phone holster at his hip like a gunslinger checking his six-gun. "My escrow closes at four and I was thinking about heading back right away. I don't want to leave you stranded if you get any legitimate offers on the Porsche."

She sighed. "I don't see that happening anytime soon." Sadly, the promising sale she'd been counting on had fallen through. Since then, the only responses to her online ad were from scam artists. "Unless I was dumb enough to take a foreign cashier's check with extra money to cover the cost of overseas shipping," she said, shaking her head. "Do they think everyone who is trying to sell a high value item is so desperate they'll fall for that kind of crap?"

Jack shrugged and shook his head. "Sometimes people believe what they want to be true. Given the market, maybe you'd be better off putting it in storage, too."

She'd considered the idea but that would mean taking out a loan to buy another vehicle. Something she was loath to do. "Maybe I should move in with Mom for a couple of months. Do some temping. Until I've saved enough to pay cash for a car."

Her brother crossed the room. "Listen, Rae, I know things are going to be tight for a while, but I really hate seeing you doubt yourself," he said, resting his hand on her shoulder. "You need to make a clean break. I'll loan you money if you need it."

She made a face. "You bought a new house and sank a bundle into remodeling. Plus, you're getting married and opening a new business, Jack. I'm not about to ask anything from you. Except maybe a reference. From your wife-to-be."

He cocked his head. "What do you mean?"

"I want Rufus Miller as my first client. Based on the two birdhouses I sold within hours of putting them in the window of Native Arts yesterday, I think the market is ripe for his kind of art—humble, hopeful and affordable. All he needs is the right Web site and a higher online profile. Which is where I come in."

Jack's jaw dropped. "You met Rufus Miller? He spoke? Really? Kat made him sound like Howard Hughes."

"He struck me as shy and slightly mistrustful. But he seemed fond of Kat. Maybe she could put in a good word for me."

Jack thought for a moment. "I'm sure she would. But do you know if he can *afford* to hire you? You can't build him a Web site for free, and is he even computer savvy enough to process orders and do all the peripheral stuff that comes with online sales?"

Good questions she didn't have answers for. But she planned to find out. "I don't know. But I have another potential client in mind, too." She grinned at him. "You."

"Me?"

"Yes. Your new dental clinic is going to need a Web site. I have some ideas about making it more interactive and drawing traffic. Would you like to hear them?"

"Now? Shouldn't I get the place open for business first?"

She lightly touched his shoulder. "It's never too soon to think about marketing." She was only half-teasing. "But I didn't bring it up before because I know how busy you've been."

He nodded. "I'll make you a deal. I'll give you free rein with my site if you promise to think about coming to work for me. You'd be great as my office manager. You'll keep me profitable, and I'd like to do some pro bono work the way Dad did." He winced slightly. "Only smarter. You know what I mean."

She did. Their father's passion of helping underprivileged children made him an easy target for an unscrupulous family. The betrayal had hurt a thousand times more than the loss of business and damage to his reputation.

"I do. That's great. I'll pitch in any way I can. And knowing I have a Plan B makes this whole move a little less terrifying. But I promised myself a fresh start doing something I think I might be pretty darn good at. If I don't try, I'll always regret it."

Jack looped one arm around her shoulders and gave her a squeeze. "I hear you. Now, let's get this show on the road. What's going with you and what's going into the storage pod?"

She looked around. "The moving company's check-list recommended keeping out any personal items I can't live without for three to six months."

"Then, you start sorting. I'll—" He was interrupted by the jingle of the phone at his waist. He whipped it from the holster and put it to his ear. "Hello? Mac. What a surprise. What's up?"

Mac McGannon was Libby's brother. Char had given Rachel the lowdown on all of her Sentinel Pass friends. Since Mac and his daughter, Megan, lived nearby Libby's guesthouse, Rachel assumed they'd meet soon enough. She half listened as she dumped the contents of her bedside drawer into the open box. She'd left the tape downstairs so she folded the flaps inside one another to create a makeshift lock.

"Really?" Jack exclaimed. "That's great. Sure. Give him my number. I think she'll be very interested. Thanks for thinking of us. And tell your sister I look forward to seeing her soon. 'Bye."

Jack flashed his big-brothers-rock grin and said, "Mac's mechanic friend in Loveland has a car for sale. A four-wheel-drive Ford Explorer. Needs tires, but it's in excellent shape and he'll make you a great deal as a favor to Mac."

She pushed the box toward the center of the room, undecided about how to label it and whether or not it should go into long-term storage.

"Are you interested?"

"If I can afford it, yes. But I can't do anything until I sell the Porsche."

Jack groaned. "Forget about the Porsche. It's winter. Unless you can find a buyer in Florida, it's going to be a tough sell. I'll lend you the money. I know you're good for it. If you like the Explorer when we look at it, we'll give Mac's friend cash."

"Are planning to rob a bank?"

His grin was almost blinding. "No, dummy. I'm getting paid for my house today. Remember? So what do you think?"

She smiled weakly. "I think it's a good thing Mom is in Florida."

His laugh sounded wry and carefree. Far different from the Jack she'd known most of her life. The serious, almost dour orthodontist who never made a move without consulting his day planner.

She wanted to drink from the same well of happiness, but his had a name: Kat. And making sure their wedding came off without a hitch was Rachel's first order of business once she got settled in Sentinel Pass. Well, right after nailing Rufus as her client.

Jack returned a moment later, a dozen flattened boxes under one arm, tape, scissors and a roll of newsprint in the other. "Ready?"

She opened the double doors to the huge walk-in closet that was now half-empty. She stood there a moment, remembering what it had been like to share space with another person. The man she thought she loved.

Jack must have sensed her pain. He tousled her head in a big-brother gesture. "Forget the golf jerk. You're moving to Sentinel Pass, the swoo center of the earth. If you're open and receptive, the right person will find you."

Swoo. She'd heard Kat mention the word, but since love, lust and sex were not part of her current vocabulary, Rachel had put any thought about the future—beyond her business dream—out of her mind. Her lip curled in a snarl. "Well, thanks to Trevor, I'm currently closed and unreceptive. So, tell your swoo to stay the hell away from me."

She thought she came off sounding tough and belligerent, but Jack merely rolled his eyes. "Right. Like any of us has control over who we fall in love with."

A swift jolt of panic grabbed her around the throat. "We do, Jack," she insisted. "We must. I have to believe I've learned from my mistakes. Real love is slow and steady, not flashy and all for show. If it isn't, I don't want anything to do with it." She gave him a stern look. "Now, can we drop the subject? New car. New business. Living out of a suitcase. Isn't that enough for one person to handle at a time?"

"I suppose. I just want you to be as happy as I am. If I see any opportunity to play matchmaker, I'll take it."

She grabbed the scissors and carefully snipped a hunk of tape. "You might want to talk to Mom, first," she said, eyes narrowing. "She tried picking my Mr. Perfect and we both know how well that turned out."

Her reply seemed to give him pause. "But Sentinel Pass doesn't have a golf course. That has to count for something."

She laughed, of course. It was either that or cry. And she'd done enough of that after Trevor left. This was her fresh start and she planned to make the most of it.

"Yo, RUFUS. ARE you home?"

A man's voice was faintly audible over the din of barking. Rufus could go for days without hearing another human voice. He had his art, his music, his dogs. He didn't need more. Or so he wished.

"Damn," he muttered, getting to his feet.

His workbench was a mess, but the good, creative kind of clutter that often led to inspiration. He rarely cleaned it off for fear he might miss something.

He hated to be interrupted and his dogs made sure nobody got close enough to sneak up on him. Clive, his regular letter carrier, had learned the hard way not to get out of his postal vehicle until Rufus was present. Rat-Girl, Chumlcy and Fred were shoulder-to-shoulder, barking incessantly when Rufus ducked through the door of his shop and started toward the center of the turnaround, where Clive was waiting.

"What now?"

Clive had been delivering to Rufus for years. He didn't expect courtesy. Heck, in the early days, Rufus took his cues from Clive, who knew this country better than anyone. Clive was only a few years older than Rufus, but he seemed ancient and entrenched—two things that would have spelled death to the man Rufus used to be.

"You gotta sign for this," Clive said, holding a letter with a green label attached to it.

Damn. Another one. The registered letters started arriving several months earlier when the genius behind Rufus's carefully designed stock portfolio was arrested for running one of the largest Ponzi schemes in history. Rufus had realized in a heartbeat that his days of hiding in the mountains and living off his investments were over. If he didn't start making money again, Stephen's House would never be completed.

He scribbled his name across the bottom of the form. The gesture reminded him of a time when he'd been asked to sign autographs by breathless young women who would have done anything he asked. Anything. And more often than not he did ask. Why not? he figured. "We all gotta die someday. So you might as well live it up while you have the chance," he used to pompously spout.

His unwritten credo. One he'd applied to the max— right up to the day his doctor said, "R.J., I hate to have to tell you this, but you have skin cancer."

Melanoma. An unremarkable word with remarkable power.

"I heard you put some of your birdhouses down at Char's place," Clive said, ripping the green card off the envelope.

"What about it?"

"Nothin'. Just makin' conversation. Heard she's hooked up with a guy from the Rez."

Something in the man's tone told Rufus the word was meant as a slight. Rufus didn't like gossip—especially the narrow-minded judgmental kind.

Before Rufus could say so, Clive added, "You know she went to California all of a sudden and put the sister of Kat's new guy—the dentist—in charge of the store. Pretty crazy, don't you think? Handing over your business to a stranger just like that?" He snapped his fingers for emphasis.

The dogs started barking again.

Clive clapped his hands over his ears. "Noisy bunch."

Rufus didn't say anything more so the mail carrier shrugged and put his truck in gear.

Once the man was out of sight, Rufus walked across the central square toward his house, which sat on a slight knoll. He'd planned to put in steps and maybe a sidewalk at one time, but then figured why bother? More to shovel in the winter.

Always conscious of the position of the sun, he hurried to the roughly hewn steps of his front porch and sat, stretching out his legs. There were patches of snow under the trees and in the shade but his south-facing home was warm and pleasant. He scooted backward slightly so his face and hands, the only parts of his body not covered by clothing, were in the shade. His thick beard would protect his face, but the skin around his eyes was vulnerable, as were the backs of his hands.

All three dogs looked at this proximity as a chance to vie for their master's attention. He rubbed, hugged, patted and got licked more than he wanted. The smell of wet dog fur was strong, but it beat the contact high he sometimes got from the glue and sealer he used on his projects.

He set the mail aside and hunched forward to scrape a spot of glue from his fingertip. After his encounter four days earlier with Rachel Grey—the woman he assumed Clive had been talking about—Rufus had returned home surprisingly energized. Her praise and enthusiasm for his work had been infectious. New ideas had flooded his brain and he'd worked almost nonstop, taking short naps on the sofa near the wood-burning stove in the shop.

He hadn't realized how much he needed to hear an

outsider's affirmation that his work had value. He was looking forward to showing her the new three-story model that he'd decorated for the holidays, using dried berries and garlands woven of pine needles.

He'd stayed away from making any more of the freeform birdfeeders that Kat and Jenna Murphy had claimed carried sexual connotations.

Yes, they'd sold well. But they weren't his favorite to make. Each one required him to think back to a dark, turbulent time in his life when sex was his recreational drug of choice. His new life was far more subdued and—he believed—real.

"Okay, guys," he said to the dogs. "Break time is over. I've got three more houses to finish before tomorrow."

Because tomorrow he was meeting with Rachel Grey again. She'd sent word via an e-mail to Char that she would be in town by then and would he mind meeting her at Libby's guest house? Char had given him the message when he returned to Native Arts to pick up his check for the two Dreamhouses, which had sold.

Since Rufus didn't have Internet service at his cabin, he'd gotten in the habit of checking his e-mail twice a week at the Sentinel Pass Civic Center. The producers of the TV show *Sentinel Passtime* had donated half a dozen computers for the townspeople to use. Rufus's occasional sales through craigslist and eBay had doubled his contact with the human population, but he knew his exposure would be even greater if he agreed to hire Rachel.

He was pretty sure no one would ever make the connection between R. J. Milne and Rufus Miller, a name that combined his maternal grandparents' surname and his childhood dog's moniker. Enough time and distance separated his current life from the flash-in-the-pan fame that had burned brightly then disappeared from sight... and memory.

He gave each dog one last pat on the head. "Whew, guys. Wet dog smell. It's going to be a long winter if I have to share a bed with you."

Not that that was likely. His sleeping quarters were in the loft and, so far, none of his motley crew had learned to climb a spiral staircase. But the nights were getting longer and lonelier. Maybe he'd end up downstairs with them.

The sad thought made him frown, but he quickly pushed it aside and took in a deep breath. Positive thoughts were good medicine. He'd learned that a long time ago and still believed it.

He rubbed his hands together, partly to warm them up and partly in anticipation of starting his next Dreamhouse. He was pleased with his recent creative flow and wondered if Rachel would be impressed.

"Whoa." He stopped abruptly, causing Fred to plow into his leg, nose-first. The dog let out a yelp of protest that made Rufus kneel. "Sorry, buddy," he said, rubbing the homely dog behind his wide square head. "I don't know what got into me. Since when do we care what anybody thinks?"

The answer was never. Giving a damn about other people's opinions had nearly killed him. He'd made supreme efforts to get past that form of egoism.

And he especially didn't care about a woman whose agenda he didn't completely trust. He'd meet with her. He'd listen to her business proposal. But he had no intention of trying to conform his work, his art or his very specific goal to her idea of success.

R. J. Milne would have bent over backward to meet her needs—especially if those needs served his own—but Rufus hadn't been that guy for a long, long time. Thank God.

CHAPTER THREE

RACHEL'S PULSE WAS jittery in a one-too-many-cups-of-coffee way, but caffeine wasn't the reason for her nervousness. Meeting her first potential client was. She wanted to appear cool, calm and professional. She felt anything but.

"You can do this," she murmured softly as she turned off her new, extremely used Ford Explorer. She'd bought it two days earlier. Yes, it had a gazillion miles on the odometer and it needed tires, but the engine was sound and the price was right.

Her Porsche was in storage, along with all of her belongings, save the boxes stuffed into the luggage compartment behind her. She'd arrived in Sentinel Pass too late last night to unpack more than her suitcase and her laptop.

She stretched across the console to grab her purse, and a piece of paper caught her eye. She snagged it, too, and sat back.

Jack's handwriting on the back of a bank deposit slip.

You're gonna rock Rufus's world. Go for it.

She smiled. Her previously self-absorbed, somewhat diffident brother continued to surprise her. Maybe there was hope for their mother, as well.

"Doubtful," she muttered, opening the door.

Her laptop was behind the driver's seat. She wrapped her hand around the handles of the leather satchel and squared her shoulders to face the Sentinel Pass Community Center. To her left was the green, slightly goofy, pony-size dinosaur named Seymour. She gave him a little wink as she passed.

A blast of warm air hit the instant she opened the door to the brightly lit reception area. She could see the computer area to her right.

She nodded at the woman behind the information desk. A large I Heart *Sentinel Passtime* pin with the name *Marva Ploughman* rested on her chest. She scrutinized Rachel as if she might need to give the police a detailed description at some later date.

Rachel's chin rose defiantly. "I'm looking for Rufus Miller."

"Oh," the woman grunted and pointed. "In there. Been pacing like a cat that's short one litter box."

Maybe that meant he was nervous about their meeting, too. Rachel hoped so.

He wasn't pacing when she found him, though. He was standing beside a window, gazing outward. She hadn't realized until that moment how tall he was. And she couldn't remember now why she'd thought he was fat. His upper body seemed disproportionately large compared to his lower half, but that might be due to his numerous layers of wool and flannel. She felt a tiny bit of sweat form on her upper lip simply from looking at him.

"Hello. I hope I'm not late. None of my clocks can agree. I think there must be some kind of time warp in this part of the mountains."

His head swung her way, and she was struck again by the odd feeling his heavy beard was fake. She'd stood close enough to him the last time they talked to know better, but a part of her would have given anything to see him beardless.

"I got my e-mail up for you to see."

No small talk. Okay. Two could play at that. "I entered your name in one of the search engines and only six entries came up. All related to your online sales. That's not good."

"More than I thought there'd be."

"When I set up your site, I'll do some key-word research to optimize your site's presence in the big search engine's organic search results. After a few days, we'll probably be looking at multiple pages of entries. First step toward making Rufus Miller a household name," she quipped.

His pale skin went a shade whiter.

"Just kidding," she quickly added. "My job is making you accessible to people who didn't even know their lives were incomplete without a Rufus Miller original. How far we take that depends on you. Demand depends on supply to keep the wheels of the economy greased. And you're only one person, so I expect the demand will exceed your output."

"You sound happy about that."

She nodded as she set down her bag and withdrew her computer. "I am. Scarcity will keep the price up and that's a very good thing."

He pulled out a chair for her. "How much will this cost me?"

While she waited for her laptop to connect with the public Wi-Fi, she pulled a file folder from her bag.

"Since I'm new to the business, I decided to offer you a flat rate for a new Web site. Then, once we've agreed on a finished product, you can hire me at an hourly fee to maintain the site. Processing sales would fall into a different category. I'd be happy to help you set up a flow chart. Or maybe you have an office manager to handle that."

A low, rumbling sound filled the air around them. He was laughing, she realized a moment later. The vibration passed through her chest and left her a little breathless. "I make the damn things. That's all. Kat helped me sell a few, but she's too busy to do that anymore. That's why you're here. How much do you charge?"

"Good question. How 'bout we work that out as we go? I promise to be fair. I'm not trying to scam you. If you had DSL where you live, I could work from your place, and then you could be sure you were getting your money's worth," she said, returning her focus to her screen.

"Kat mentioned something about a satellite."

"Do you want me to find out about it?"

He hesitated. "Maybe."

She motioned toward an empty chair. "Have a seat. I'll show you a few mock-ups. These are simple, simple prototypes. If you like any of the ideas, we'll start there and build a more personalized site. If you don't, I'll bring you some more choices in a day or two. After I've unpacked."

His head lifted and he looked out the window. "You bought a new car."

She thought she detected a hint of approval in her choice. "Used, but functional."

He didn't speak again until she started showing him

the ideas. The first three were met with silence, but not a condemning air. "I like this one," he said when she pushed the arrow key for number four.

Her personal favorite. The background was a generic mountain scene with a giant coniferous pine in the center of the page. "There are several ways to showcase your work in the foreground. The navigation buttons are on top. I left a spot for your photo right here," she said, pointing to the screen.

"No."

"Okay. You can keep it on your personal page then."

"No photos of me. Period."

"But people will want to know that you're real. That this isn't a mass-market hoax. To paraphrase from *Field of Dreams,* 'If you build them, people will come to your Web site.' They'll want to be part of your online community, and they'll need to put a face with your name."

He shook his head. "Either the pieces sell on their own merit or they don't. Nobody's gonna buy one because they saw this mug. In fact, it might scare them off."

She would have agreed if she hadn't spent the past few days obsessing about him. True, he resembled some people's image of Bigfoot. But in her mind, that over-the-top rugged backwoodsman look was sexy—and very marketable.

But she sensed she'd have to handle this part of the negotiations delicately. "What if we used a group shot of you and the dogs? More dogs than you."

His lips pulled to one side. "Maybe. I'll have to ask them."

"Excellent," she crowed triumphantly. "I have the

release forms right here. A single paw print will do." She waved a blank piece of paper.

He didn't laugh again, as she'd hoped, but she could tell by the glint in his wonderful, dark chocolate eyes that he wanted to. It was enough to fill her with hope. At least, that's what she called the skittering sensation that dashed up her spine.

"Time's up, Rufus," a loud, not particularly friendly voice said from behind them.

Rufus ducked his head as if the woman approaching them might recognize him. Odd, Rachel thought. Didn't everybody in this small town know each other? "I'm sorry," Rachel said, turning in the not terribly comfortable chair. "What do you mean?"

"The rules say half an hour per sign-up. Rufus's been here an hour, already."

Rachel glanced around. "Nobody's waiting."

"I gotta go some place, and I'm the only volunteer who could make it in today. I'm locking up."

Rachel wasn't always good at spotting liars, but she'd gotten better since her marriage. This woman wasn't telling the truth. Rachel could only assume she had something against Rufus. "No problem. There's Wi-Fi at the restaurant, isn't there?"

"The Tidbiscuit closes at two." The woman looked at Rufus. "You could have come in earlier, you know."

He didn't appear to hear her. He turned off the computer he'd been using and stood. The chair he'd been sitting in made a loud, screeching sound.

The woman pivoted on her heel and stomped back to her desk.

"She doesn't like you," Rachel said.

"I know."

"Why doesn't she like you?"

His lips pressed together, virtually disappearing into his beard. Rachel assumed that meant he wasn't going to answer, but when she looked up from putting away her computer, he'd bent down close enough to whisper, "I donated one of my early bird feeders to the community center. She said it was dirty."

Rachel shrugged. "They're made out of wood and acorns and stuff. Why would she expect it to be clean?"

"Pornography kind of dirty."

Rachel blinked. She tried with every ounce of self-control not to grin but her lips had a mind of their own. "How could a bird feeder be pornographic? Did you have little naked creatures doing…things?" she barely choked out.

She looked up. His lips were present again. They were tweaked in the most gorgeous way. A smile that magically reached his eyes. Her laugher died the moment some other emotion took hold.

Lust.

No, no, no, she silently cried. *Nope. Not that. They're lips. That's all. Nothing magical and sexy about them. Nope. Lips.*

Then the lips spoke. Low and private, for her ears only. "There were two pieces of wood. Yin and yang. I found them separately and put them together. I hung it from the eaves out there to attract birds."

Trying to picture what he described didn't ease the sexual fission she was experiencing one bit. "Do you still have it?"

He nodded. "I took it home when the mayor gave it back."

Rachel reached out and touched his arm. "Please tell me she's not the mayor," she whispered, nodding toward the woman shooting them the stink eye.

His thick mop of hair shook back and forth.

"Whew." She pretended to wipe her brow. "I would have had to move before I unpacked."

There was a look of approval in his eyes. "Listen, I'd really like to go over this proposal as soon as possible. Is there any way we could continue this at your place? I have four-wheel drive now. I could follow you home."

He moved his shoulders uneasily and turned to start toward the door. The mean lady was nowhere in sight, thank goodness. Rachel didn't want to fake a thank-you.

He opened the door for her—a courtesy she hadn't expected. That and the pulling out of her chair added up to lovely manners that didn't quite jibe with his back-woodsiness. If there was such a word.

"Where are your dogs?"

"Home. The little one got her foot caught in a tangle of branches and needed to rest. She can't control herself in the truck, bouncing from window to window, afraid she's going to miss something."

"So you left all three of them at home?"

"To keep her company."

To keep her company. She was touched more than she thought wise. Maybe they should put this meeting off a day or two. *Or ten.*

"I walked in. To town," he added as if she were the

simple one. "I guess I could ride back with you. Probably the only way you'd find the place."

She swallowed, loudly. "Okay, then, let's…go."

WHAT AM I DOING? Rufus silently asked himself, not for the first time since climbing into her vehicle back at the civic center.

It wasn't as if she'd put a gun to his head. But something about this woman played havoc with his usual self-restraint. People thought he was shy, when in truth he simply didn't want to connect with anyone. And he was damn good at avoidance.

Until today.

Maybe it was her earnestness. Or her chipper can-do air. He'd replayed their first meeting at Native Arts in his mind way too often over the past few days. He'd been bracing for this get-together with equal parts anticipation and dread. And now, for some inexplicable reason, he was bringing her home.

Not a single, non-four-legged entity had entered his inner sanctum—his studio. Not that he called it that. He preferred the term "workshop." Even though he associated that word with Santa.

"Why would someone buy a birdhouse for a Christmas gift?" The question had been bugging him ever since she suggested they had to jump on creating an online presence to make the most of the holiday market. "Aren't they more of a summer thing?"

"I don't think so. Besides, it's always summer in some part of the world."

The world? Come on, he silently scoffed.

His art wasn't for the masses. In fact, he knew from experience most consumers preferred generic, mass-made crap to something that made them think. Time and again as a model he'd been told his look was too different, not boy-next-door enough. Of course, they never complained about the view of his backside. Provocative seemed to work when you were selling men's bikini briefs.

"Why me?" he asked, after pointing out the mostly invisible fork in the road. No signs or numbers or cutesy flags to announce his place in the world.

"Pardon?"

He could tell by the look of concentration on her face she wasn't completely comfortable driving the bulky vehicle. The Explorer was a huge leap in size and maneuverability from the Porsche. He wondered if she resented having to downsize in style because of her divorce. Assuming, of course, that was the reason, he reminded himself. What little he knew of her came from an online snippet he'd found before she arrived at the community center.

"Why pick me for your first client? I'm not gonna make you rich."

She glanced sideways, her smile wide and filled with irony. "Oh, don't worry. I don't expect that. I've been rich—for a brief moment in time—and a wealthy lifestyle is not all what it's cracked up to be."

He blinked in surprise. He agreed, but the sentiment was not shared by very many people. He doubted if she really meant it. Probably she was still bitter about her divorce from some big-name golfer. Rufus had never heard of him, but the guy's press agent had done a pretty good job of making his client appear the victim of his blinded-by-love impulse to marry Rachel—a woman who "didn't understand the complexities of the professional athlete's life." Or some such baloney.

"Your road doesn't see a lot of action, does it?"

The innocent remark triggered an odd reaction somewhere in his libido. He'd seen more than his share of action in his twenties. Enough to last a lifetime, he'd thought, but suddenly he felt the old juices stirring.

"Just the mailman," he answered, forcing his mind to stay focused. "Once or twice a week."

"Well, that's going to change," she said with conviction.

Rufus swallowed and shifted to look out the window. He'd known any increase in sales would necessitate logistical changes. He simply hadn't extrapolated every ramification. Her earlier comment hit home. It wouldn't take a very large jump in sales to make his current system of handling every aspect of the transaction himself impractical and obsolete. He'd need help. And for the short term, at least, she seemed the best person for the job.

But he needed to do this on his own terms. As a model, he'd been tossed hither and yon by the demands of his profession. By the mere nature of the job, he was a commodity. That mind-set took a real toll on a person's self-worth—even if that person was in demand and at the top of his game. It wasn't surprising how many people in his profession had suffered breakdowns and burnout. Many self-sabotaged through drugs or alcohol. He'd gotten out in time…but not by choice. That's why he planned to established concrete boundaries with Rachel right from the start.

"My place is just ahead. Better slow down. The road gets a little rough."

Her laughter was unexpected and it caught him midchest. "It's going to *get* rough? I love it." She beamed happily. "We honestly could play up the yeti factor in your Web design."

He wondered if he should feel insulted. "What's a yeti factor?"

"This," she said, making a global gesture. "Think about it. You live alone in the deep woods of the profoundly spiritual Black Hills. You create amazingly unique pieces of art from natural materials found in your world. You are an enigma. Larger-than-life, but rarely spotted by regular folk. Like the yeti."

She braked hard to creep over a pothole, gripping the steering wheel with both hands. As the SUV lumbered across the section of washboard, she shot him a quick glance. "This is a good thing, by the way. It sets you apart from other artists. They call it branding."

He silently cursed. He knew all about branding. He'd lived by the brand, and damn near died by it.

"Like Greg Norman, the Shark? Or the Grey Pearl?"

She slammed on the brakes, tossing him forward and back against his seat belt. "I beg your pardon? Were you checking me out online before I got there today?"

He nodded. That's where he'd seen her ex-husband's excellent Web site. He didn't know if it was Rachel's design or not, but the home page featured the tanned, blond poster boy for pearly whites, which the site had cleverly explained was how he earned his nickname. *Always smiling Trevor Grey is a positive force on the course,* a caption below the guy's headshot had claimed. To Rufus, the man's warm blue eyes—probably computer enhanced, in his opinion—lacked any real depth. The guy reminded Rufus of a store mannequin selling golf shirts and accessories.

As the car continued to idle, she gave him a thorough once over, as if seeing something different in him all of a sudden. "Smart move. As I said, I did the same with you. And, to answer your question, yes. Trevor's nickname plays on his natural charisma. Also, pearls connote success, achievement and warmth." She stepped on the gas, muttering softly, "Two out of three ain't bad."

He wondered what someone as real and independent as Rachel saw in someone so contrived and artificial. If he had to take a guess, he'd say fame. One of his least favorite words. Fame corrupted. Ninety-nine percent of the time women bought in to a certain image and didn't ask questions. Until later.

Did that make them shallow? Not really. The truth was he never let anyone see any deeper than the image he projected. Maybe the same was true of Rachel and her ex. He didn't know and he didn't really care. She'd gotten under his skin but that didn't mean their professional relationship would lead to anything else.

He had a feeling she was intuitive enough to see beyond the image he projected for the world, and he'd deal with her questions as best he could. Was he ready for a full disclosure show-and-tell? Hell, no. In his opinion, there was nothing more pathetic than a former overnight sensation or one-hit wonder trying to make a comeback. His past was done and gone. He'd pretend to be a yeti before he'd dig up the pictorial remains of R. J. Milne.

A loud, passionate chorus of barks shook him out of his reverie.

She rolled down her window an inch. "Wow. You have fans. With good ears," she added. "We must be getting close."

Fans. He'd had a fan club. Once. A long time ago. "See the break in the trees?" he asked, leaning forward to point the way. "They weren't happy about being left behind." He moved impatiently, anxious to check on the animals. "I hope Rat isn't bouncing off the walls. Her foot was pretty swollen this morning." He'd almost taken her with him to see the vet but decided to give her body a day to heal itself. He was proof that self-healing worked in certain circumstances.

The tires made a crunching sound as the car turned onto the gravel he'd had delivered a month or so earlier.

"Pull up to the front," he said. "I'd better check on her."

He jumped out as soon as the vehicle came to a stop then hurried to the front door, which was unlocked. "Hello, doggies. How's our girl?"

Rat spring-boarded into his arms and licked his neck while the other two dogs milled around his knees, eager for reassurance their master was back to stay. She seemed fine, but he carefully probed her paws. "Much better," he said, kissing the foot she'd been favoring that morning. "Come and meet a new friend."

Friend? Not so fast. He didn't have friends. Except for the canine kind.

Determined to reestablish the boundaries he felt most comfortable with, he let the dogs perform their usual scary, step-one-foot-out-and-we'll-bite-it-off routine. Showing more courage than Clive, she opened the driver's side door a crack and put her bare fingers within nipping range. "Is it safe to get out? They sound like they want blood. Mine."

"This is them happy," he admitted.

She made a face. "Then I don't want to hear them mad." She got out, but didn't move from the spot as the dogs pushed in to get a good sniff. "Nice doggies," she said, patting Chumley's broad head. "Big doggie."

Rufus suppressed a smile and snapped his fingers to bring the oldest, most well-trained dog to his side. "Fred, sit. Come here, Miss Rat."

All three animals obeyed, which cleared a path to the front porch where he was standing. The walk wasn't exactly shoveled because it wasn't exactly a sidewalk. He gave her credit for wearing proper snow boots, but the morning sun had melted enough to make it slippery.

"I can see why you said I'd never find the place," she said, looking around. "Gives new meaning to the term 'out-of-the-way.'" Her tone was more amused than irked. "With a road like that one, I bet your mailman loves you."

"Gives him something to complain about."

Fred trailed behind her, the hair on the back of his neck standing at attention. Rufus didn't understand why until Rachel turned slightly and he spotted the mock fur trim around the hood of her white down jacket. To Fred, it probably looked like a cat ready to pounce on him.

"Fred," he warned, "stay."

The dog's powerful haunches hit the snow-covered ground. "Good boy."

Rachel took a deep breath of fresh, frosty air. "It's really beautiful here," she said, twirling suddenly, as if untethered from some invisible leash. Her shoulder-length red-brown hair danced in the breeze. The small, stylish sunglasses she'd worn while driving were pushed to the top of her head, giving him a clear view of her eyes. And the charming array of freckles on her nose.

He had to physically clamp down on his impulse to yank her into the shade, even though the early afternoon sun wasn't much of a threat since it was already sinking behind the pines.

She's not me, he reminded himself. Every person's skin was different. A few freckles didn't mean she'd wind up with cancer.

Still, he couldn't prevent himself from clearing the distance between them to take her elbow and hurry her along. Three quick steps and they reached the safety of the porch. She appeared a little bemused by his rush but didn't comment. Instead, she exclaimed, "Wow. This is a real log house, isn't it? What did you use for chinking?"

"Cement with plastic filler."

"Does it insulate?"

"Stops the wind."

She walked to the wall between the large picture window and front door and ran her bare hand over the yellowish cedar log. "Gorgeous," she said. "Do you mind if I take a picture?"

Hell, yeah. "Why?"

She already had a small digital camera out of the enormous satchel slung across one shoulder. "I figured you'd want a page on your Web site about you—the artist. This house is a work of art in and of itself." She pivoted on her heel before he could reply and charged to the far end of the porch. "Ohmygod, look at these wind chimes. Did you make them?" She lightly fingered the interlocking puzzle pieces he'd carved out of wood. A shiver passed down his spine as if she'd been touching him. "Of course, you did. I can see your hand in it. Do you have more? I bet you could sell a million."

He shook his head. "Someone could replicate this in China for twenty cents. Each one took me hours."

She put her camera to her eye and snapped a few shots. "Exactly my point. There will always be cheap imitations, but what you're selling is authenticity. The more you charge, the more the buyer respects you."

That would have made him laugh, but he actually understood what she was saying. At the height of his modeling career, he was getting paid an obscene amount of money for doing practically nothing. Strutting. Pouting. Looking haughty and unattainable. The more he charged, the more the magazines and art directors wanted him.

"Tea?" he asked, suddenly needing to slow things down. The sound of a camera clicking made him uneasy—even if the viewfinder wasn't pointed his way.

"Sure. That would be great. Can I leave my stuff here a minute?" she said, dropping her tote bag to the seat of the Adirondack chair he'd made a few years ago. "I forgot something in the car. I brought your dogs a treat."

He paused, his hand on the door. That was a word his animals knew well. Before he could utter the command to stay, all three were on her heels, yipping with excitement. He walked to the top step to make certain they didn't trip her.

She managed fine, softly chattering to the dogs. Each animal appeared to be captivated by this new, very friendly person. Even Chumley, the most dignified dog Rufus had ever met, panted with ecstasy when she patted his head and neck.

She opened the driver's door but slammed it a second later and flat-footed it to the back of the car. He frowned, noticing the ice under her feet.

She heaved open the rear hatch. Her vehicle was angled so he could see the layers of boxes stacked irregularly on top of each other. She'd meant it when she said she was still in the process of moving.

With hands on her hips, she made a sound of impatience that carried all the way to the porch. He liked the way she expressed exactly what she was feeling. He envied that honesty.

Her audience waited with rapt attention. Rat-Girl stretched to place her front paws on the bumper. Rufus snapped his fingers. "Down."

The little dog obediently lowered her butt to the snow while shivering with what he was pretty sure was excitement, not cold.

Rachel pulled two boxes off the top of the pile and set them to one side, then climbed partway into the car. Through the side windows he could see her stretching for something.

A few seconds later, she let out a triumphant cry. "Found it."

As she wiggled backward, her jacket rode up and Rufus got one quick glimpse of her shapely waist. She landed on the ground awkwardly, her foot tangling with some loose tape attached to one of the boxes.

Rufus had already started forward to help, when she caught her balance. Muttering something about "bad packers," she shook her head. When she realized he was only a foot away, she made a face. "Jack helped me load stuff. And I specifically told him to put this box in

storage. I wonder how much other useless cra— um…
stuff is in here."

He started to offer his help but she stopped him. "I'm
good. Really. Simply wrestling with the reality of being
footloose and fancy-free." She faked a smile. The first
he'd seen that wasn't real. "Here," she said, holding out
a crumpled bag adorned with multicolored paw prints.
"Doggie treats. Organic. Sprouted grains. I bought them
in Denver."

His heart melted into a puddle in his chest. She had
absolutely no way of knowing about his health issues
or the fact that he'd gone on a macrobiotic diet after his
diagnosis. Although he'd gradually reintroduced more
normal foods into his diet, he still tried to eat healthy,
organic ones when possible.

"Thank you."

"You're welcome."

He stuffed the bag in his pocket, intending to pass out
the treats once he'd helped repack the boxes. But when
he bent over, he realized that something looked off-kilter.
"I hate to tell you this, but your rear tire is almost flat."

"What?" she yelped. "No way."

She let go of the box she'd started to pick up. It must
have been fairly light because it tumbled over on its side.
"Oh, no," she cried the moment she saw the state of her
tire. "Jack tried to talk me into getting new ones before
I left Denver, but do you know what I said? I said, 'I
prefer to buy local.' How dumb is that?"

He didn't think it was dumb. "Do you have a spare?"

"I have no idea. But I do have auto club. I'll call—"
She stopped at his look. "No cell service?"

"It's only low, not flat. I have a portable compressor.

I'll top it off before you leave. I'm sure you'll get back to town safely."

"Really? Cool. Then, let's go inside and talk business before…before…" She'd turned to finish picking up the boxes but something stopped her.

Rufus glanced around. "Uh-oh." He put his hands on his hips. "Fred," he boomed. "What have you done to Rachel's…um…sex toys?"

CHAPTER FOUR

RUFUS LEANED DOWN to pick up the object Rat-Girl had dropped beside his booted foot. The handle of the hot pink whip was as long as his forearm but tapered to a fine point, which was adorned with ribbons and brilliant purple feathers. He couldn't have been more surprised if a marching band of elves had suddenly appeared.

He cleared his throat and picked up the gaudy, over-the-top instrument of…um…pleasure? He hated to admit he wasn't sure how it might be used, but his initial impression of Rachel had changed. And a certain part of him could even envision testing out the silly thing. With her.

"Oh, my," she said, her gaze following as a couple of bright feathers drifted to the snow.

"Sorry," he said, handing the whip to her, blunt end first, as if it were a knife or a loaded pistol.

Her chin rose with a kind of dignity Rufus admired, but her attempted smile betrayed her. "Faulty packing. That happens when you hire family," she said, a little hitch in her voice.

He was a single step away from her. Even in the dry, cold breeze, he could smell her. Not the cedar, pine, dog and earth scents he was most familiar with, but something fresh and feminine that he realized with a start he'd been craving. Their gazes met and held for what seemed too long. Especially given the objects scattered around them.

He was the first to move. He started toward the wreck of a box, intending to cram anything and everything inside. She jumped sideways, arms out, to block his efforts. "No. Please. I'll do it. This is so embarrassing. When I see my brother…"

Words spilled out of her mouth at a rate Rufus's brother would have called super-soundic. Even as a little kid, Stephen was always making up new words.

He gave a mental shake to return to the moment. *What part of this situation made me think of Stevie?*

Farce. Stephen had loved gross-out comedy. The more inane the better. Their parents had hoped he'd outgrow it. Unfortunately, he never got the chance.

Rufus was stuck in memory lane when he heard her low "Uh-oh." Her inflection sounded pained.

Since she'd positioned herself to keep him from seeing the worst of the spill, he had to peer around her to discover what unspeakable horror had her momentarily frozen in place.

"Yowch," he said, one hand dropping to his groin without conscious thought. "I'll replace it."

At the horrified expression on Rufus's face Rachel wasn't sure whether to laugh or pray for the earth to open up and swallow her alive. *It* was a sixty-five-dollar, nine-inch, all-too-realistic-looking dildo that Rachel had unwrapped at her bridal shower to the jeers and cheers of other party-goers. "Trust me. It's better than the real thing," one woman had proclaimed. Her friends and coworkers had even named it for her. Dexter. After the HBO serial killer with a conscience.

At the moment, Dex was giving extreme pleasure to the dog with the big, squarish head. Fred, she believed. And Fred was chomping on the pliable, lifelike rubber with such gusto his master actually looked pained by the image.

She fought to contain the laugher that started bubbling from that horrible well of inappropriate responses that her ex-husband had hated so much. But she simply couldn't it hold back. Within seconds she was doubled over, howling. Tears—the Chris-Rock-on-a-roll kind—obscured her vision and she actually had to grab Rufus's arm for support until her ab-scrunching guffaws diminished.

"Oh, wow," she said through her sniffles. "I needed that."

She released her grip and dug a tissue out of her pocket to blow her nose. "Did I leave my camera in my briefcase? Damn. That would go viral on YouTube."

He seemed to question the humor of the situation, although he didn't say anything. His reaction was probably normal. Hers was probably not.

"It was a gag gift at my wedding shower."

"A *gag* gift? No pun intended?"

The joke jolted her. It was so unexpected and quick. Another facet of this complex and interesting man she hadn't picked up on when they first met. She decided to test her theory by sharing something she hadn't even told her brother. "My ex-husband hated that thing. He called it an affront to the moral integrity of society and the sacred vows of our union. He ordered me to get rid of it. Not asked. Ordered."

Rufus gently but firmly shooed away the little dog when she—Rat-Girl?—tried to get a piece of the obscene chew toy. "And…"

She shrugged. "I'm cheap. Excuse me. I meant to say thrifty. I buried it under some other stuff in a drawer. I'd planned to re-gift it. But before I could, he trashed our *sacred vows of union* in a far more obscene and public way."

His wooly eyebrows asked the question his lips failed to voice.

"He got caught boinking another golfer's wife. Oops." She put her icy fingers to her mouth, mockingly. It suddenly struck her how cold the air was. She hadn't noticed until that moment. Before she could suggest they move this circus inside, Rufus bent and rather daintily picked up the dildo. The dog released it without hesitation.

He held it up so they could both examine the very comprehensive distribution of teeth imprints. "There was a time when I would have paid good money to see my husband looking like that. The teeth marks, I mean," she interjected. "Size-wise…let's just say it's under-standable why he felt threatened."

Rufus looked at her a moment. "Where do you want this?"

She shrugged. "Keep it. Your dog seemed to like it."

He shook his head slowly from side to side. "No, thanks. I don't want to give them any ideas. They already outnumber me."

She knew he was joking. The dogs seemed as well-trained as any she'd ever met. She'd begged Trevor for a puppy, but he'd told her—wisely, it turned out—they weren't ready for that kind of commitment.

Rufus quickly gathered up the remaining toys, stuffing everything into the box. She didn't see what he did with the gnawed dildo but assumed it was in the box, too. She appreciated his efficient, unflappable calm.

"So, how 'bout that tea? And, no offense, but I'd prefer you didn't take any more photos without asking first."

She didn't get why, but she shrugged. "Okay."

As she passed in front of him, she heard his deep intake of breath. "Are you sniffing me?"

He stiffened as if poked. "Trying to place your perfume. Lavender?"

"Dryer sheets."

"Grapefruit?"

She blinked in surprise. "Shower wash. That's a pretty acute nose you've got there. Acute. Not a... cute...nose."

He put his hand to his face. "You don't like my nose?"

His little insecurity made him a bit more human. Not that she really considered him a yeti or Bigfoot's younger brother, but he kept himself so detached and watchful it was hard to get a real take on him.

"It's very nice, from what little I can see. I don't mean to offend, but you are the most hirsute man I've ever met. From the neck up, anyway. Good insulation in the winter, huh?"

Instead of responding, he led the way to his house and opened the door for her. She picked up the rest of her gear that she'd set on the beautiful, handmade chair, and hurried into the warmth. "This is nice," she said, rubbing her hands together to get the blood circulating. "That cold sort of sneaks up on you. Mind if I look around?"

Hell, yes, he minded, but he couldn't say that. He'd

invited her inside and was about to hand over the pro-
verbial keys to his business. He needed to feel her out,
see if their work ethics would mesh, get on the same
page business-wise, and all that other big-world drivel.
Either that or he showed her to her car and said,
"Thanks, but I've changed my mind."

The words were on the tip of his tongue, but out of
habit, he reached down to empty his pockets. Something
he did every time he came inside, because very often
whatever he'd happened to pick up served as inspiration
for his next art project. This time his hand closed upon
a paper bag.

He pulled it out and suddenly found three eager faces
looking up at him. He opened it. "Well, what have we
here, my friends? One for each of you."

Tails were wagging as he passed out the treats. Rat
trotted toward her pink dog bed—the one concession to
femininity in the otherwise manly furnishings. Fred
devoured his in a single gulp. Chumley walked to his
spot by the back door to enjoy the goodie at his leisure.

"Thank you," he said, looking across the room.

"You're welcome."

Kind. Direct. Nice. Thoughtful.

The adjectives were piling up. Instead of asking her
to leave, he walked into the kitchen and filled his copper
kettle from the filtered water spigot beside the sink.

While the water heated, he surreptitiously followed
her as she explored his home's open floor plan. The
building was a simple square, not unlike his birdhouses.
But his design included a spiral staircase leading to a
second-floor master bedroom, reading nook and bath.
A four-foot closet jutted into the room adjacent to the

main door to give storage space and definition to the dining room—a place he kept filled with potted plants in the winter.

"Your home is really beautiful, Rufus. Unique and not the least bit Spartan."

He opened a cupboard to grab a couple of mugs to keep her from seeing him smile. He wasn't surprised that she would have assumed he lived in a cave. He did project that image. For a reason.

This land had been in his family for sixty years or more. As a child, he would spend a couple of weeks every summer here with his parents and his younger brother. The original cabin had been tiny and poorly maintained. No indoor plumbing and a hand pump for water.

By the time he inherited the place, the house had been past the point of reclamation. He'd saved as much of the original wood as possible and used it to build his workshop. He liked to think some of his inspiration came from the good memories the wood held of his childhood.

"And impressively green, I might add," she said, bending to examine the fireplace insert that proudly boasted its environmental compatibility. "You're neat, too."

He dropped a tea bag into each mug.

She put her hands on her hips and turned in a slow circle. "My ex couldn't be in a hotel room for half an hour without turning the place into a pigsty. But look at this. No clutter. I'm impressed. Are you gay?"

Rufus nearly lost his grip on the handle of the kettle and upset one of the mugs when he overcorrected.

"Oh, sorry," she said, hurrying across the room.

"Complete lack of tact. I didn't mean to sound judgmental. Neatness is a good thing. Just ask my mother."

He heard more than she probably intended in that statement. He finished pouring the steaming water over the tea bags then returned the pot to the stove. "No. I'm not gay," he said, sliding one of the mugs across the marble countertop. "My father had his doubts, but not because of my fastidiousness. Purely habit and my mother's influence. She was Betty Crocker personified."

"Why did your dad question your sexual persuasion?"

Rufus chose the simple answer. "I never married. Real men got married and had kids. Period."

"Why didn't you? Marry."

There was no simple answer to that question, but he'd been asked often enough that he had a pat answer. "Too busy. How's the tea?"

She picked up the mug and brought it to her nose. "Smells good. Is that…grapefruit I detect?"

Damn. He liked her. How did that happen? "I don't think so."

"Good. I'm not fond of citrus in my tea. Never got that whole lemon-and-milk thing. I went to London and Scotland on my honeymoon. My husband was busy golfing most of the time so I did the tourist thing. Scones and clotted cream…now, that's a different story."

He motioned for her to join him at the breakfast nook. It wasn't the warmest spot in the house, but she must have been comfortable since she'd dropped her jacket over the back of the sofa.

Rufus noticed Rat-Girl sniffing it, so before joining her, he picked it up and hung it in the closet. When he returned to the table, she had a bemused smile on her face. "Apparently I picked up a few bad habits in the short while that I was married."

He was curious about that, but decided not to ask. Better they kept things impersonal and professional.

"How long have you lived here?"

He'd known that kind of question would come up eventually, so last night he'd decided on a proactive approach to dealing with any personal queries. "Here's a bio you can use," he said, pulling a folded piece of paper from the chest pocket of his wool shirt.

She blinked in surprise. "Wow. You did this?"

He nodded. He wasn't computer illiterate. He'd owned state-of-the-art technology at his flat in New York. He'd had cell phones for as long as they'd been around and could text with the best of them. He'd sold the majority of those toys when he moved here, knowing it would be years before he'd have Internet access in this remote corner of the world. Still, he had a laptop and printer in the second-floor office above his workshop. He rarely used either machine, but, thankfully, there'd been enough ink to print a couple of copies.

She sipped her tea as she read. She only glanced around the edge of the paper twice to look at him. He wondered which of the not-quite lies gave her pause.

"Nice job. I can use this." She sounded disappointed.

"Good."

They drank their tea without speaking, the low hum of the refrigerator and the occasional grunt or squeak of the dogs the only sounds. He waited, knowing the rather large gaps in his bio would probably drive her mad until she asked.

"New York, huh?"

He nodded. He couldn't *not* mention his time in New York but he'd reduced his twelve years to a single line. "After a successful career in New York, Miller retired to the Black Hills to pursue his art." Simple. Worked for him.

"You don't care to mention what kind of successful career you left behind?"

"No."

"Too bad. People will be tempted to fill in the gaps. Taxi driver. Actor. High-rise window-washer."

He shrugged. "Street sweeper. Gigolo. Falafel maker. Underwear model. Take your pick."

She cocked her head. "Do they still have street sweepers? Oh, sure, the guys in the big trucks. I was picturing you with a broom. Didn't fit."

He couldn't see that image, either, but probably for different reasons. "The past isn't part of who I am now."

"Sure it is. It shaped you."

He fought the urge to touch his ear, where a large hunk of flesh and cartilage was missing. Not noticeable given his current hair style and beard, but gone all the same. "Perhaps, but it's nobody's business. Either they like my work enough to buy it or they don't. Who cares what I did for a living?"

She held her hands out and made the universal gesture of *who knows?* "We can try it your way. Secretive might be a good thing. Especially given your street-sweeper-gigolo-falafel-salesman past," she added with an impish grin.

He waited for more questions. She sipped her tea and looked around, smile still in place. That was easy, he thought. Too easy.

"So…" She let the word trail on for several seconds. "Are you ready to show me your studio?"

He didn't answer right away. He hadn't thought that far ahead in this process. He'd known he would have to show her at some point, but this soon?

"It's messy. Sawdust everywhere. The glue is probably carcinogenic and I only have one respirator."

"Did you use glue this morning?"

He shook his head.

"Then, it's probably safe, don't you think? I won't stay long. Just snap a couple shots—if you say it's okay. I didn't get a chance to photograph the two pieces you left at Native Arts. They sold too fast."

The glue excuse was weak at best. He didn't work with anything toxic, but the tung oil he used to protect the wood was a bit stinky. "Okay," he said, fighting the desire to call the whole thing off.

One quick peek. If she hates the Dreamhouses, then I can say I tried and call the whole thing off. And as much as he needed her to like what he'd been building because if she liked them other people—buyers— might, too, a part of him hoped she hated them. The risk of failure was far higher than it had been when only his body was on the line.

She chugged down another swig of tea then jumped to her feet. "Great. Let me get my camera. For my own reference," she quickly added. "Before we go live, I'll see about getting each piece professionally photographed. If it's cost effective. Don't worry. I'll handle everything."

Don't worry, R.J., I'll handle everything.

His brother's last words. How could he not worry?

CHAPTER FIVE

RACHEL PUT ON HER JACKET, which Rufus held for her. Once again she was struck by his old-world manners that seemed at odds with his lumberjack persona. And who in the world could have predicted that he'd hand her a surprisingly articulate and polished bio?

As he stooped to pet his dogs—all three had rushed to his side the minute he approached the door—she could sense his apprehension. Maybe insecurity was intrinsic to all artists. She'd been a nervous wreck the first time she tried her hand at Web design.

"How do you heat your workshop?" she asked as they stepped outside. The wind had come up and a biting chill turned her jeans stiff and icy cold.

"Solar and wood. I like the quiet when I'm working."

Trevor had been the exact opposite. He'd wanted nonstop distractions—music, TV, iPods, cellphones—even when he was golfing. That alone should have been an immediate red flag when she'd try to reach him and he wouldn't pick up her call. Silly trusting girl, she'd come up with every excuse but the right one.

"How long have you been doing this?" she asked, shivering at the crunch of the snow beneath her boots. A wide path had been neatly shoveled at one time, but she could see the crisscrossing trails of the dogs and probably deer that had caused the sides of the snow banks to crumble.

"Can't remember, exactly. Started dabbling. Out of boredom, mostly. Wind chimes were first, then bird-houses, and, lately, Dreamhouses."

"But no more X-rated ones." She couldn't deny she was a little disappointed.

He didn't answer. Instead, he opened the large metal door of a surprisingly modern, surprisingly big building that seemed more like a warehouse than an artist's studio. The vertical metal siding was a dark green color. Except for the small overhang above the door, the entire wall was plain. No windows. No signs.

She stomped off her boots on a bristly wire mat and hurried inside. Her still forming criticism about working in a tomb died unspoken as she looked around. The wall to her left was almost entirely glass. Overhead a dozen or so optical enhancing tubes made the most of the cloudy sunlight. Like his home, half of the second floor was living space, directly above two partitioned-off rooms. Unlike his home, a regular staircase, probably six or seven feet wide, provided access to the loft area.

"Well, look at this. I'm impressed. I've been in some pretty amazing homes, but I don't think any could claim a better view. Now I see where you get your inspiration."

She wasn't inspired to take off her coat, though. It was cold inside.

"I banked the fire this morning and haven't been back," he said, directing her with one hand at the base of her spine toward a small orange glow at the far end of the building. Her first thought was a sleeping dragon, but common sense told her she was seeing a wood-burning stove. She wished he'd hurry up and add some logs.

"This is where I work," he said, nodding toward the larger of the two partitioned areas.

The walls between the two unique spaces were sliding barn doors, she observed. He could deconstruct either room with ease. *Clever.*

"I haven't been able to stop thinking about your Dreamhouses, Rufus. In photography they call that one perfect image the money shot. That's where the money is going to be."

"Birdhouses take less time *and* less material. That means they'll sell for less."

She turned to face him. "But birds don't have disposable income. Dreamhouses sell something everyone needs—hope. Or maybe you could combine the two ideas. Help a bird in need while generating good karma for your own dreams."

She couldn't tell by his expression whether he was poised to laugh or roll his eyes. He did neither. He hesitated a moment then crooked his finger at her to follow into the heart of his lair. Wood smells—cedar, redwood, cherry and who knew what else—filled her nostrils.

"Kat helped me sell most of my early stuff, but I kept the one that the mayor gave back. I'm not sure why."

A slight catch in his voice made her question that assertion but she didn't say so. She took a step closer. Their arms touched momentarily before he leaned across the wide, messy workbench for an object tucked behind a stack of neatly planed pieces of wood.

She blamed the odd surge in her heart rate on curiosity, not proximity, but she shifted sideways a step to give them adequate nontouching space. A faded T-shirt with a vaguely familiar logo was draped across the two-foot-tall object. She tilted her head to read the print but before her brain could come up with the connection, he whipped off the cover, balled the fabric between his hands and tossed it over his shoulder.

She might have commented on the gesture but words left her. Excitement, laughter, surprise—she wasn't sure which of those feelings best summed up her first impression of the object. An unusual work of art, for sure.

"A woman's body and yet...it's not."

Suspended above the horizontal piece by microfilament fishing line was a phallic-shaped hunk of wood that fit perfectly against the V-shaped opening. "And that hunk of wood is male...and yet, it's not."

She looked at him. "You carved this?"

He shook his head. "Mother Nature did most of the work. I found the two pieces miles apart. Picked them up because they were interesting. Then when I got back here and dumped everything on my workbench...I tried arranging things. I didn't have any real idea in mind, but these two fit together."

Her mouth seemed strangely dry and she had to make her gaze leave the erotic tangle of wood. "But you carved the rest of it."

"Shaped. Sanded. Whittled. The moss, I added. And the dried buffalo berries."

Nipples. Ruddy and erect. She swallowed and tried to clear her throat. "Were the ones you sold similar?"

He nodded. "After I finished this one, I started looking for pieces of wood that had a certain look. Some were larger. Some smaller."

She finally understood why the lady in town was upset. These *were* erogenous sculptures, not birdhouses by anybody's standards. She was turned on and wished she wasn't. Her reaction was completely unprofessional. *As long as he doesn't know I'm turned on, I can still pull this off.*

She moved at the same time he did and they touched. Again. Through multiple layers of clothing. But Rachel swore she felt it all the way to her core. Her happy place. Which, frankly, hadn't been happy in much too long. For so long, in fact, she was actually envious of a hunk of wood.

"Sorry. Want to see my new stuff?"

"Yes, please," she answered, trying to stifle a moan of relief when he pushed the sexy carving out of sight.

As he moved past her, she had a good look at his profile. Chiseled. Hawkish nose. Thick eyebrows that matched his bushy beard. She'd never kissed a man with a beard and couldn't help wondering what it would feel like. Soft? Bristly? Scratchy?

Unfortunately, she'd probably never know. At least, not with him. It was one thing to have unprofessional thoughts, quite another to act on them. Her mother would die if she ever found out. "Is there a bathroom I could use?" she asked. "That tea went right through me."

He pointed to a door across the room.

As he watched her walk away, he unconsciously licked his lips. His imagination wasn't dead. He'd read her face the moment she touched the piece. Same reaction he'd had when he first stumbled across the half-buried hunk of wood. He remembered tripping over an exposed branch. Instead of tossing it to one side, he'd picked it up, turning it this way and that. When he'd run his thumb over two perfectly placed bumps he'd heard a voice in his head say, "The spirit of a young woman lived in this tree. Her soul mate is up ahead."

Chumley found the matching piece. Weathered by the elements. Smooth and so obviously phallic Rufus had laughed out loud. It hadn't taken a huge leap to imagine the two pieces together.

After that first find, he'd gone hunting for more. They'd sold like first edition Beatles cards.

He was sitting in front of the woodstove when she returned. "Can I ask you something? Why did you stop making the sexy ones? They're very unusual. I'm sure there's a market for them."

Should he tell her the truth or make something up? The truth was simpler, if emasculating. "When you live alone, it's not a good idea to spend all your time making erotic sculptures out of wood."

Her eyes went wide and her cheeks turned a tiny bit rosier. "I get your point. My panties are a little damp from one look, I can imagine—" She stopped abruptly. "Tell me I didn't just say that out loud."

He might have let her off the social gaffe hook but his brain had stalled at *damp panties* and his body's automatic response made it hard to think. *Hard* being the operative word.

"I'll show you the Dreamhouses," he said, getting to his feet a bit awkwardly.

He walked fast to put some distance between them. By the time she caught up, he was safely behind the table he'd set up to handle the shipping part of his business.

"What's that smell?" she asked.

"Tung oil. I use other products, too. Depends on where the house is going. Indoors or out." He grabbed the closest one. "I'm not a trained carpenter. I don't start with a plan."

She looked surprised. "How do you know how to build it?"

There was enough in his process he couldn't explain that he was a little superstitious about discussing it. "I start with the walls then try to picture someone living in it. That's how I realized there was a spot in the middle that was completely wasted space."

She pulled it close and peered down the chimney. "And you came up with the brilliant idea of making it a place to store your secrets, your most private dreams, your rants you want no one in the world to hear."

He wouldn't have put it quite so eloquently, but that pretty much summed up the theory behind them. "I have a few one-story models. I call them starter houses."

She studied one of the small ones. "The front and back porches could serve as bird feeders. And if you left the door off, there might be room for a nest, right?"

He could see where she was going with the idea. "Yeah, but the center core is where you drop in your notes. If I take that out, no more Dreamhouse."

She nodded with enthusiasm. "Oh, I know. I don't want you to change that aspect. I was thinking more along the lines of dual functionality. We market to the dreamers and the bird lovers. You have this unique place to store your secrets, plus you help a bird family in need."

He scratched his head. "Oh." He wasn't sure how he felt about that.

Her hand was shaking when she set it down. She leaned

closer and inhaled the unsealed cedar chip shingles. "I think your work is amazing, Rufus. Beautiful and unique. I can't wait to get to work on your Web design."

The positive reinforcement was better than the praise he used to garner from the toughest photographer. Unfortunately, he knew that praise could be addictive. His overinflated ego had blinded him to some of the worst choices he ever made in his life. He wasn't going that route again.

"How many can you sell?"

"How many can you make?"

He thought a moment, calculating what he guessed he could accomplish with the stockpile of material he and the dogs had picked up during the summer and fall. "Fifty a month, max. But I have sixty already made."

As she looked at him, he could almost hear her brain working. They both knew nobody was going to get rich from those kinds of numbers, but he gave her credit for not flinching. Instead, she said, "I know your overhead is low at the moment, but there will be some initial start-up expenses with the site. And we'll have to factor in monthly maintenance costs for updates and newsletters once we have a mailing list. Have you thought about whether or not you're going to hire someone to handle shipping, returns, processing credit cards, online payments and whatnot?"

His stomach tightened. Those were all things he'd done his best to avoid thinking about over the years. "Will I wind up making any money?" He had to. That money had a very specific purpose.

"Of course. Because we're going to charge a lot, and I promise to keep my costs down in return for your favorable testimonial on *my* Web site." She grinned. "Don't worry. I'll write it for you."

"Will you make any money?"

She hopped up on the table and crossed her legs. "I'm not trying to get rich off you, Rufus. I don't need a lot at the moment. Libby's guest house is free because I'm watering her plants and keeping an eye on things at the big house. The main reason I'm so anxious to do this is for the exposure."

"I don't know anybody. I can't talk you up."

Her smile looked indulgent, but her tone was patient. "All I need is one success story, Rufus, to sell myself and my skills. I'm not promising this will be fast or easy. I'll be learning as we go, but I feel confident I can do this job for you. Despite what my mother thinks."

"Does it matter?"

"Does what matter?"

"What your mother thinks."

She heaved a great sigh. "One would certainly think not, but one might be wrong. She's a numbers kind of person. Creative things make her nervous. I make her nervous."

He didn't see the connection.

"I went into accounting because that made her happy. She'd been through a lot with my dad dying and some crummy stuff that happened with his business. I wanted her to be happy and not worry so much. But I discovered that I wasn't happy unless I was doing artsy-fartsy kinds of things." She stuffed her hands into the pockets of her jacket and shrugged. "I was in charge of all the parties at my former job. Name a theme, I'd throw a party around it. And that included building Web sites to announce it, organizing blogs, online invitations, guest lists, videos, photo albums and way more stuff than you want to know."

He understood the corporate mind-set that spent big bucks on showing off. He'd been the guest at those kinds of parties for years.

She misread his frown. "I know that sounds frivolous and not at all the same as building a commerce Web site, but I honestly think I can do this, if you'll give me the chance."

Her earnestness was hard to resist, but he hated the idea of being someone's—anyone's—guinea pig. He'd left his fate to chance often enough in the past, but this time he had other people depending on him. "A month."

She blinked in surprise. "Pardon?"

"If I haven't started to show a profit in a month, I hire someone else."

Her pretty lips pursed in thought. "Well, this is retail's make-or-break season. If I can't sell those puppies—" she pointed toward his inventory of Dreamhouses piled around them "—before Christmas, then I might have to eat crow and admit that my mother was right."

He could tell the idea didn't appeal to her, but she straightened and looked him in the eye. "I'll do your Web site completely on spec. If nothing sells, you're not out a penny. If you make bank, then you pay me for my time. How's that sound?"

Like the best deal he was going get. "Okay."

"I don't have a contract for you to sign. That's still on my to-do list. Can we can shake on it?"

Rufus didn't need anything in writing. His investment broker had provided him with reams of official documents, and the jerk had still managed to screw Rufus and thousands of other investors out of every dime they gave him. He extended his hand. "Don't waste too much time on the design. They might not sell."

She squeezed his hand without any girlish hesitation. "You're wrong, Rufus. The key to getting people to part with their money is going to be in the presentation. We have to give them hope without promising them anything."

He was glad to hear her say that. He didn't want to deal with irate customers who didn't win the lottery after filling one of his Dreamhouses full of "I will win the big one" wishes.

"When do we start?"

"Right now," she said, slipping off the table. She rubbed her hands together. "Could you put another log in the stove? I'm going to take pictures, make notes and start developing ideas for the layout."

Now?

She apparently heard his silent cry. "Sorry. Much to my mother's chagrin, I'm happiest when I'm planning a new project," she told him. "Mom would say that's because a new crisis keeps me from finishing my old ones."

Her mother didn't sound anything like his. Mom had encouraged him to be anything he wanted to be—even an underwear model.

"Do you have a desk I could use? Or even a flat surface away from the dust. I don't want to disturb you, and I don't want to mess up my laptop."

He motioned for her to follow him to the far end of the building. His favorite overstuffed recliner sat at an angle a few feet from the wood-burning stove. His dogs were already in place, waiting for him.

"Will this work?"

She put a hand to her heart. "It's perfect. If I had a Dreamhouse, I'd wish for some place just like this."

He couldn't tell if she was serious or playing him. He hated to be played. "I have work to do," he said, pivoting on the heel of his heavy hiking boot.

He almost said, "Make yourself at home." But he caught himself in time. She wasn't his guest or his girl-friend. He needed to remember that.

CHAPTER SIX

"WHADDAYATHINK? DO I group all the Christmas stuff together or sprinkle it throughout the shop?"

Rachel had stopped at Native Arts before heading up the mountain to Rufus's cabin. She had the route down pat since she'd been there twice that week, but even with four-wheel drive—and new tires—the road was an adventure.

She had some time to kill because she'd learned all too quickly that she and Rufus kept different schedules. She was early to bed, early to rise—like her mother. Rufus hadn't come right out and forbade her to enter the workshop without him present, but he had made a point of telling her that he often got so caught up in his work he didn't turn in before the wee hours of the morning. She took that to mean she needed to "chill," as Char's son, Damien, liked to say, and accept the fact that she could not control every aspect of every day. Not to mention the fact that she'd learned straight off that if her client growled like a hibernating bear awakened too early, it was very likely that she wouldn't get an answer she liked anyway. So, she was determined to adapt her schedule to his, and it wasn't as if she didn't have an abundance of other things to do.

"And good morning to you, too, Char. I'm fine, thank

you. And, yes, I would love to discuss holiday displays with you. Already today I cleaned my house top to bottom and I shoveled every inch of sidewalk around both the guest cottage and the main house." A small storm had deposited about a foot of fresh white powder.

"Busy girl. But did you finish the book club book?"

Rachel frowned. "I started it."

"And…"

"I'm struggling to keep my head in the story." Mostly because of a certain completely-not-her-type mountain man. Granted she was in the process of developing a Web site devoted to the guy and his art, but still Rufus Miller occupied way too much space in her head at the moment.

"Understandable," Char said. "You do have a lot on your plate. Are you here to talk about the wedding?"

"I have a few details to go over, but in answer to your question," she said, dropping her briefcase beside the desk, "I'd say you need both. A central display will give walk-in traffic an immediate feel of the holidays. But by tucking holiday items in unexpected places, people will respond subliminally to the challenge of the scavenger hunt. Within reason. Keep it obvious, but fun."

She demonstrated by moving a small wooden display shaped like a Christmas tree to a spot beside the hanging dream catchers. The sunlight from the overhead skylight caught the crystal beads of the snowmen earrings and made them appear to dance.

"Wow. That's cool." Char put her hands on her hips and faced Rachel. "Are you positive I can't hire you to manage this place for me? I'll throw in all the venison you can eat. I have a connection."

Rachel was happy to help her friend from time to

time, but she wasn't ready to bail on the idea of being her own boss. "Thanks. I'll keep the offer in mind if things don't pan out with my first client." She said the last with a little squeal of delight that made Char laugh.

"I can't believe you talked Rufus Miller into moving into the twenty-first century. Honestly, for a long time I wasn't sure he had all his marbles, but Kat calls him a gentle soul hiding from a troubled world. *That* I can understand."

Rachel wasn't completely convinced Rufus had moved forward. He continued to place intense restrictions on what she could and couldn't put on his site. Her mother was the queen of micromanagers, but even she knew when to let the person she was paying to do a job do that job.

But she didn't tell Char that. Every business that involved working with the public presented its own unique challenges. She and Rufus would strike a happy medium soon. She hoped.

"Do you mind if I check my e-mail while I'm here?"

"Go for it." Char motioned her to the area behind the desk, where a computer and printer sat alongside a surveillance monitor that showed four unique views of the operation. There weren't any customers present because Char didn't open for another half hour, but on one of the screens Rachel spotted a person moving around.

Someone's in the teepee, she realized.

Native Art's large white teepee was a focal point that was hard to miss if your destination was Sentinel Pass. Due to the cost of heating it, the teepee didn't see a lot of use in the winter. "Who's that?" she asked, pointing to the screen.

"Damien. He's home today with a cold, but he likes to hang out in there. Says it helps put him in touch with his Lakota roots." Char sounded both pleased and a little bemused. "Those heaters William brought for the wedding work fabulously, by the way."

Rachel was glad to hear it. "Great. That reminds me, do we have a final tally on the head count for the caterer? Last I heard Kat's brother and his daughter were a possible maybe."

"Put them down as a yes. Cade and Shyloh are moving back from Texas as we speak. Kat's excited to have them closer, although she's a little worried about Cade working for her dad again. Old family dramas, if you know what I mean."

Jack had mentioned a few things about Kat's strong-willed—some said megalomaniacal—patriarch on their drive to Denver. That conversation, of course, had led to a rehashing of the sad, excruciating experience with their father. Jack's perspective was slightly different than Rachel's since he hadn't been living at home at the time of Dad's death. Granted, he'd been privy to the catalyst that, in effect, killed their dad, but he didn't share Rachel's memory of watching their mother carry on with her life as if it was business as usual, while Rachel watched her father wither and die.

"I'll put them on the list. From what Jack told me, I was prepared not to like Kat's dad, but I have to say, the two checks he's sent for wedding *folderol*—his word, not mine—have been very generous."

Char's gaze lingered on the screen where her son was sitting, a buffalo robe across his lap. He looked up at the camera, suddenly, as if sensing their appraisal, and flashed a peace sign.

Char gave a little laugh. "He knows I watch him. I can't help myself. I'm like a first-time mom with an infant...who can read and argue politics. Amazing."

They talked a few minutes longer about kids and wedding plans. Rachel answered a couple of e-mails from her mother. Nothing important, but questions that would earn her a lecture if she didn't respond. One gave her pause, though. "My mother wants to know if Rufus is a hermit or a recluse? Is there a difference?"

Char thought a moment. "I'm guessing you have to be rich and famous to be a recluse. So, that would make Rufus a hermit."

Rachel quickly typed in Char's answer, adding: "Unless he's secretly rich and famous."

Char must have been reading the screen as Rachel typed because she burst out laughing. "Right," Char said dryly. "So. Seriously. Are you sure you don't need me to do anything for the wedding?"

"Not a thing. We're talking only sixty guests. I was in charge of organizing my former company's holiday parties for three hundred."

Char made a face that clearly said that kind of job was not her thing. "Hey, could you watch the store for a few minutes? I'm trying my hand at making homemade chicken soup for my sick kid. I left it on simmer, but I don't trust my stove." Char's home was directly behind the store.

"Sure. No problem."

Alone with just the hum of the computer, Rachel clicked on a popular search engine and typed in *rustic birdhouses*. Rufus had yet to give her an exact price for his pieces. If she had an idea what the competition was selling for, she might be able to help Rufus place a dollar value on his.

She was completely engrossed in her search when she realized she wasn't alone. A jolt of awareness made her fingers freeze midsentence. She looked sideways. "Oh. Hello. I didn't hear you come in. Sorry. Can I help you?"

The soft-stepping customer was a woman. About Rachel's mother's age. Short, steel-gray hair messy from the wool cap she was holding. "Yes. Thank you. I want to look at the spears you have over there. I was in a couple of days ago and took one of the artist's cards. I checked out his Web site, but I didn't see anything I liked better than the ones you have. So, I decided to purchase it in person. You'll take care of the shipping, won't you? It's for my grandson in Virginia. His birthday, not Christmas."

Rachel leaped to her feet. She was familiar with the spears because she'd handled another sale while Char was gone. The man had required a few changes from the artist, Carl Tanninger.

"How old is your grandson?" How did one diplomatically tell a customer with ready cash that a historical replica of a spear was not a toy.

"Forty-three, I believe. I can remember the day and month of my grandchildren's births but never the year."

Rachel stifled a sigh of relief and grabbed the key to unlock the safety chain around the display. "How many grandkids do you have?"

"Four. And two great-grandbabies. I love my children, but, everything you've ever heard about grandparenthood is true. Love 'em and leave 'em with their parents. That's my motto." She winked elaborately then added, "Michael is the oldest. He lived with me and my husband nearly every summer while both of his parents were working. He's a dear man and very good father. He and his wife love Virginia Beach, but I always hear a twang of nostalgia when he asks about South Dakota. He'll love having this to hang on his wall."

Rachel helped the woman—Jan Knutson, she learned after introductions were made—find the right spear for her grandson. The most expensive one of the bunch. As she rang up the sale, Rachel asked, "Is the reason you don't mind spending that much money because it's such a unique piece?"

The woman signed her credit card before answering. "Yes," she said, carefully balancing the intricately carved shaft between her outstretched hands. "It's a work of art. Michael knows and appreciates nice things. And every time he looks at it, he'll think of me. And the Black Hills. That's a wise waste of money, don't you think?"

Rachel finished typing the mailing address in the proper form and hit Print. Char would carefully box the spear and call for a pickup when she returned. "Not a waste at all. I agree with you completely. I asked because I'm starting to market some rather unique art pieces for a client." She caught herself before she said friend. *Where did that come from?*

Jan looked interested. "What sort of things?"

"Dreamhouses. He combs the hillsides looking for natural materials that he incorporates in each piece. At the center of each house is a chimney. You write your dreams on a slip of paper, roll them up and tuck them away."

"How intriguing," the woman said. "Do you have any here? My youngest granddaughter is graduating from high school this coming spring. She's next to impossible to buy for."

"Put your e-mail address on the back of my card," Rachel said, quickly digging one out of her bag. "I'll send you photos and a price sheet. If one strikes your fancy, I'll bring it here for you to look at before you buy."

"Wonderful," Jan mumbled, pawing through her purse for something. "Here. This is my son's card. He and his wife publish a monthly magazine that focuses on local businesses and people of the Black Hills. My daughter-in-law writes most of the articles. She might be interested in doing a story on the artist. Have him give Jim a call."

Rachel felt a familiar inner buzz that told her things were falling into place. The organizing problem-solver in her loved the feeling and couldn't wait to share it. She checked her watch. Still early by Rufus Miller standards, but surely he'd want to hear that the universe was starting to align in his favor. With luck—and a little free publicity—orders for his Dreamhouses would soon be rolling in.

RUFUS KNEW THAT TAKING a morning soak ran a certain risk. Despite his pointed hints to the contrary, Rachel's exuberance for life and passion for her job ran contrary to his schedule.

"I'm not a morning person," he'd told her.

"You're not that much of an afternoon person, either," she'd retorted cheerfully.

She was always cheerful—morning or evening. Chipper. Vivacious. Positive. Optimistic.

All things he wasn't. Had he ever been that hopeful, he wondered, carefully lowering himself into the oversize copper bath he'd ordered from a specialty company when he first moved into his house.

The cabin was equipped with a very nice, tiled shower in the master bathroom, but Rufus's idyllic vision of living in the mountains had always included being able to soak in a tub in front of a roaring fire. With the help of specially adapted hoses and an in-tub heating system, he could do this with very little mess. His contractor had even included a cleverly disguised drain in the wood floor so the gray water could be filtered and reused to water plants.

Rufus loved his tub. It was where he achieved his best meditation.

He'd set an alarm clock this morning for the first time since moving to the Hills to be sure he could bathe in peace and privacy. He wasn't sure how Rachel had talked him into giving her a key to the house—or had it been his idea?—but she'd made it a habit to stop at the house before heading to the workshop. She said she liked to touch base with him without having to talk over the smell of glue and tung oil.

He turned his chin and looked at the poinsettia plant she'd brought him the day before. Variegated red and pink with green lower leaves. A bright and festive addition. A nice gesture. Unfortunately, the plant made Rufus more aware of the fact his home never changed with the holidays. The question he couldn't shake from his mind returned. When had his life become so stagnant?

"Damn," he muttered. He took a big gulp of air and sank down so his head was completely under the water.

Eyes closed, he tried to block the image that popped into his head.

Rachel.

Awake. Asleep. It didn't seem to matter. She was omnipresent.

Understandable, he told himself. She was a huge presence in his life, these days. She was a giant agitator shaking up the status quo. Pretty flowers were the tip of the iceberg. She brought fresh ideas, too.

"I really think you need a Facebook page, Rufus. Online social networks are great for passive PR. You start by connecting with classmates, old friends, business associates from your past. Before long, they'll buy a Dreamhouse and recommend you to all their friends."

He lifted his chin to suck in a gulp of air. His knees were cold. It crossed his mind that he should have added another log to the fire.

Oh, well, where was I…? Facebook. Yeah, right. Like that's going to happen.

"What about a blog?" she'd proposed the day before. "You wouldn't have to type it. To start out, you could record your thoughts and I'll transcribe everything and post it for you. I think people would be interested in what it's like to be you."

"Argh," he blurted as he sat up.

The woman wanted too much from him. She was like a reverse caveman—dragging him by the hair into the twenty-first century. The changes were too dramatic and contrary to his original plan. He had to find a way to put this genie back in her bottle.

"Uh-oh. I'm way too early this time, aren't I?"

Rufus froze at the unexpected sound of a voice.

Rachel's voice. He used his fist to wipe the water from his eyes and looked toward the door. She'd only popped her head in. He gave her points for manners.

"I knocked. The dogs didn't bark so I assumed you were at the workshop. Sorry." She closed the door a little more. "I'll be down there. Bad Rachel."

She'd freeze at the shop. He hadn't started a fire, yet. If she tried to do it herself, she'd probably burn the place down. "Come in."

His tone sounded gruffer than he'd intended.

"I don't have to stay. I can come back in an hour or two."

She could. But she'd probably spend that time working on his Web site. Something he'd decided he wanted to scale back—in a big way. He had to—for reasons he couldn't share with her. He knew the news wasn't going to sit well with her.

"As long as you're here, you can wait…" She couldn't stay in the kitchen or living room. He'd grown considerably more modest than his earlier career might suggest. There was no way he was getting out of the water with her in the room. "In the loft."

His private space, but he couldn't remember leaving out anything too personal or too revealing.

Her head popped back in. "Seriously? You're sure?"

"Shut the door. It's cold."

She jumped into the room and was immediately surrounded by dogs. "Hi, guys," she said, bending to hug and pet each of them. "I guess you're getting used to me being here. You didn't even bark."

She took off her gloves and stuffed them in one pocket of her jacket. From the other pocket she withdrew three doggie chew bones.

It was obvious from his dogs' response that bribery had become routine without his knowing it. As usual, Chumley carried his treat to his large, padded bed, which Rufus had moved to the corner by the hearth. The old dog's arthritis seemed worse in the winter months. Fred disappeared as if fearful someone might try to take the bone away. Rat-Girl paraded around the tub a couple of times, showing off her prize, as if to say, "How come you never bring us presents?"

"Nice tub," Rachel said, shrugging off her jacket. She started to toss it on the sofa, but caught herself and hung it from the peg behind the door.

"Meditation."

She had to pass by within a few feet of him to reach the spiral staircase to the loft, but she politely turned her back and crab-walked, talking the entire time. "Meditation. Oh. Cool. Like some people might use yoga or a steam bath or sauna. I get it. Maybe you could blog about that."

He would have laughed at her dogged determination and single-mindedness if not for one thing. Scooting sideways, as she did, gave him the best view to date of her near-perfect butt. Firm, trim but rounded in the right places. Maybe because of his previous claim to fame— *People* magazine had named his the hottest tush in the country one year—he had a soft spot in his heart for a nice derriere. And hers was set off most becomingly by her tight tan corduroy pants, which rode low on her hips with a thin brown leather belt woven between links of gold chain. A hunter green wool turtleneck sweater had been tucked in, but presently was half-hanging out.

He felt something stirring in the warm water. He looked down. Yep. Another party heard from.

"Awkward," he muttered.

"Huh?" She paused and glanced over her shoulder. "Did you say something?"

He refused to succumb to modesty. For cripes' sake, he'd posed with a veritable G-string on in front of twenty people or more at some shoots. "No."

Their gazes met and held, but he sensed she had more than adequate peripheral vision. Her cheeks turned pink and her neck moved when she swallowed. "Oh. Okay."

Her gaze dipped for a fraction of a second then she spun around and quickened her sidestepping pace until she reached the stairs. "Call me when you're done. Take your time…um…soaking. I really am sorry about interrupting."

He leaned against the curved back and let out a muffled groan. The tone of her apology seemed to imply that she thought she'd interrupted something more than a bath. Not a one-person orgy, he guessed, but something along those lines.

A memory popped into his head. "What's masturbation?" Stephen had asked when Rufus was in junior high. Rufus had discovered girls and their father's stash of *Playboy* magazines. The combination meant long showers and the occasional locked door of their joint bedroom.

"Jerking off," Rufus had answered. He'd tried to keep things real with Stephen. Their parents weren't the type to talk about the birds and the bees, even in those euphemistic terms. Rufus remembered thinking that he was Stephen's best chance at leading a normal life when he grew up.

Unfortunately, he never got the chance. One stupid twist of fate ruined everything.

Pinpricks around the bridge of the nose made him inhale deeply and look up. To stare straight into the eyes of a beautiful voyeur.

CHAPTER SEVEN

SHE HADN'T MEANT TO LOOK—not even a teeny little glimpse—but the metal circular staircase gave her a momentary sense of vertigo. It was look around or fall sideways. And since she happened to be facing toward the center of the room when the dizziness hit, she got an eyeful.

Her knees immediately turned rubbery. Her palms tingled, making her tighten her grip on the railing. Her mouth went arid and she had to lick her lips to get enough saliva together to swallow.

Holy moly, the man was glorious in his nakedness. Stretched out in the oversize copper tub with its old-fashioned high back and rolled edges, his pale limbs seemed bigger than they should be. And practically hairless.

She leaned forward a bit, trying to make sense of what she was seeing. His bushy head of hair was slicked straight back from his high forehead. His beard seemed subdued—normal, even. But what surprised her most was the overall lack of body hair, except for a small, triangle between his amazingly well-defined chest muscles and a thatch at his groin.

Don't look. Wrong. Bad, Rachel. Stop.

Her mind refused to listen. She wasn't an expert on

men's bodies, by any means, but she was willing to label Rufus's package prime, grade-A, choice. And a lot of it.

Oh, man, she silently groaned. The dampness between her legs was back.

To distract from the obvious wrongness stemming from the instant lust she was feeling she tried to focus on the other thing that was bothering her. What is wrong with this picture, she asked herself.

"You're not a yeti," she exclaimed, a jolt of awareness surging through her body. A different kind of awareness. "You…you're a man. A regular, ordinary man." She looked at his groin again. "Well, maybe not ordinary, but you know what I mean."

He didn't fake undue modesty. She gave him credit for that. He got up with purposeful grace. Dripping like the statue of David in the rain, he leaned over and reached for the large towel hanging from the back of a chair. After slowly, casually patting away the rivulets of water on his upper torso, he braced one long, beautifully masculine foot on the edge of the tub and wiped it dry. He planted the dry foot on a bath mat and adroitly hopped sideways to repeat the effort on his left leg.

His bare derriere was a true work of art, she realized, salivating. *Look out, David, there's a new butt in town.*

Once he had the towel secured around his waist, he turned to look at her. "I never said I was a yeti."

"Maybe not in so many words, but you let people believe you were Bigfoot's close cousin. Why? Are you in trouble? Witness protection? Hiding out from an ex-wife and nine kids that you owe back child support?"

She knew the answer to that. Of course not. He was an honorable man, even if he had been—in a sense—

lying to her from the very beginning. Hiding his true self beneath layer upon layer of scratchy plaid wool.

The way her ex hid behind his charming smile. The way her father hid behind his white lab coat.

Suddenly furious—and very close to saying or doing something she might later regret—she plunged ahead up the staircase, vertigo be damned. She was three steps into the room when it dawned on her she'd marched straight into the lion's den. This was his bedroom. Yes, there was a couch and chair and reading lamp set adjacent to a built-in library along one wall, but to her left was a king-size bed with a gorgeous red silk comforter. What kind of clueless hulking recluse decorated with red silk?

And, if I'm not mistaken, real, honest-to-goodness oil paintings.

Two. Bold, impressionistic, Warhol-influenced. She couldn't name the artist, but she'd seen a similar style at a gallery in London. The price tag on each piece had made her jaw drop.

She felt, rather than heard, him climb the stairs. He was a big man. That much was true. And he must have taken sweats downstairs with him because he was dressed all in black when he reached the landing. Except for his white athletic socks. She found that incongruity reassuring.

"Who are you?"

"You've seen my driver's license. And my credit card. You know who I am."

That was true, but she could tell by the way he didn't meet her eyes that there was more to his story. "Who were you?"

His head went back slightly so he was looking down his long, slender nose at her. A tiny squiggle of memory bounced around her mind. Not someone she'd ever met. Not one of her ex-husband's friends or someone on the professional golf circuit. He didn't seem athletic enough, despite his toned body. No, but he could have been someone she'd seen.

"Are you an actor?"

He made a scoffing sound. "Good grief, no. I stay as far away from the *Sentinel Passtime* people as possible. I'm sure they're nice enough, but their energy is enervating."

Books. Art. Silk. Vocabulary words. She searched his face but nothing came to her. His beard was starting to fluff out again as it dried. His hair had filled in around his face covering his ears. He was starting to look more like the Rufus she knew.

"Listen, Rachel, I'm sorry about the peep show. I didn't expect you for a couple of hours. I needed to think, and I do my best thinking in a bath. The house design didn't lend itself to an indoor tub and I don't like the cold well enough to sit in one outside in the winter, so I had the copper tub made. I call it my Saturday night special," he said, a sort of self-deprecating humor in his tone.

She knew he bathed more often than once a week. "Today's Tuesday."

"I know. Like I said, I needed to think."

Now, the humor was gone and something faintly foreboding seemed to linger in the air. "You're pulling the plug on your Web site, aren't you?"

"Not the sales part, but everything else," he admitted.

She'd sensed his growing disenchantment with the whole online-community concept, but being Rachel, she'd ignored his concerns in favor of what she thought best for him. Shades of Mom, Jack would have said.

"Then, I guess we're done here," she said, trying to salvage a scrap of pride. She started toward where he was standing, intending to leave. He didn't need her. No one did. Not really.

"Rachel," he said, his voice low and conflicted. He stepped to the left to block her way. His large, warm hand closed around her forearm when she tried to push him aside. "You're wrong about that."

Then he pulled her to him, his arms enclosing her in a cocoon of warmth that made her think she might be in the middle of one of his Dreamhouses. Safe and secure.

His kiss was not at all what she was expecting. Soft, gentle and far too proper—at first. When she tilted her head and leaned into him, his reaction matched hers. Their tongues got involved. Their breathing changed. Her hands were touching—or were they gripping?—his massive shoulders.

She'd wanted to do that since day one. As wrong as it was, she'd never experienced anything that felt so right—even the odd cushiony texture of his beard. She wanted more. Everything. Every inch of that gorgeous body she'd seen in the water.

At what price, Rachel? Her mother's voice. *You mixed business and pleasure once before and look how well that turned out.*

She stopped kissing him.

He lifted his head and looked at her; his clear, intelligent eyes asking for direction.

"This is a bad idea. A sort of combination *Titanic* and *Hindenburg* all in one."

His head cocked sideways. "Hyperbole not withstanding?"

She adored his quick wit but she made every effort not to smile. "It's possible I've taken unprofessional behavior to a new level. First, interrupting my client's bath. Then, kissing him."

"If it's only the client thing that's bothering you, I could fire you."

"You already did that. Is making out with you my consolation prize for losing your business?"

He made a groaning sound and took her hand. "Come and sit down. We need to talk."

She started to balk, but changed her mind when it struck her that leaving with some modicum of self-respect was lost to her. She might as well hear him out and try to figure out what she did wrong.

She chose the sofa because no matter how great his body was under those sweats and how wonderful she was certain it would feel to make love with him, she wasn't strong enough—emotionally—to handle casual sex. She wished like hell she was but… "I'm sorry. I didn't mean to stare. That was rude. A total invasion of your privacy. I should have turned right around and marched—"

"Don't beat yourself up about it." He perched on the edge of the large leather chair adjacent to the sofa. His big, rough hands clasped together. "I'm not that modest. At least, I wasn't in the past. And, I'm glad you're here so we can get this ironed out."

That didn't sound as final as she'd feared. "I'm not fired?"

"No. I'm not as simple as people think, Rachel. I know I need a Web site to sell my stuff. And maybe I'd sell more if I let you plaster my face, my personal history, my—what do you call it? My blog?—all over the place. But I can't."

"Why? If you'd trim your beard a little, I bet a lot of women would buy a Dreamhouse in order to write secret wishes about you." *I know I would.*

He ran his hand over his beard, giving a little tug. "Did you ever hear about those indigenous people who refused to have their photographs taken because they thought the camera had the power to steal their souls?"

She nodded.

"Well, it's true. It happened to me. I lost myself for a dozen or so years. Coming here saved my life. Literally. If I'd stayed in New York, I probably wouldn't be alive today. I can't—I won't—risk falling back into that old trap."

She was confused. "What trap? Success?"

"It's hard to explain. Coming here was more an act of desperation than conscious choice, but living here has brought me peace. Can't we come to some kind of compromise? Find a way to sell my work, without selling me?"

She sat back and took a deep breath to slowly let it out. "It's a good thing my mother isn't here. She'd say, 'See, Rachel? This is what you do. You take an idea and run with it without looking to see if anyone is following.' "

"The way Rat-Girl teases Fred with the ball?" he asked, smiling. "Sometimes she's halfway down the road before she realizes he gave up and went home."

She could picture the scene all too clearly. "Exactly.

I have the ball, but you went home a few steps back. I'm sorry for not paying better attention."

His shoulders lifted and fell. His wide, wonderfully shaped shoulders— She coughed into her fist and blinked to refocus on their conversation.

"…you wasted time building pages or links or whatever they're called that won't be used."

She nodded. She had half a dozen ideas sketched out. Hip, fun things that she knew without a doubt he'd hate. But she also had one idea that might appeal to him.

She jumped to her feet. "Stay put. I want to show you something. It's a bit passive for my taste, but…" *But this isn't about me. Duh. This is about the client.*

Her bag was on the floor by the staircase. She pulled out her laptop and quickly returned, setting it on the narrow coffee table. The Mac booted up and she clicked on the icon she'd toyed with early in the creative process then abandoned. Maybe she should have listened a bit more closely to her muse. "It's rough. A work in progress."

Rufus turned the computer so the light from the window behind him wasn't casting a shadow. The colors appealed to him immediately. The dark greens and browns held a cool, mysterious and sensual quality. Suspended from the branches of the earthy canopy were photos of his Dreamhouses, each with a name indicating it would reveal more if clicked upon. Home. Birdhouses. Dreamhouses. Buy. Contact. FAQ.

"Frequently asked questions?" he confirmed.

"I was going to suggest using the questions I asked you the first day we met. If we keep the answers short and simple, we build in a mystery without making it obvious."

He clicked on Home.

The background was a faded blueprint. A sketch, actually. One of his early designs made to look like a blueprint. At the center was the secret room. A hand-drawn arrow with the words *where dreams are born* was penciled in red. A sidebar told the story of how the Dreamhouses came to be.

"I like this."

Next, he clicked on an image hidden in the trunk of the tree. He'd completely missed seeing the profile at first. It was labeled *Who?*

Swallowing, he braced himself for the worst. "Who is Rufus Miller?"

The question appeared to have been chiseled in wood and was superimposed over a big photo of him at his workbench. Taken from the back. The sepia tone was old-fashioned. He could have been a kid dressed up in his grandfather's coat, Santa Claus in plaid or a very husky woman, he realized.

He read aloud. "Who is Rufus Miller? Retired falafel salesman? Gigolo on the run from an irate husband? Street-sweeper with carpool tunnel syndrome?" That made him snort. "Ask the individuals who know him best."

He looked at her, questioningly. "Who would that be?"

"Click on Chumley," she said, pointing to the dog napping at his feet.

He did. A woman's voice—Rachel's, he realized—spoke. "Hello. My name is Chumley. My master rescued me from certain death. I'm the oldest member of the family and the best at finding wood and—forgive the pun—bark, which our master then uses in these unique masterpieces. Was that too many masters?"

Her face was scrunched up as if horrified by the sound of her own voice. "Too cheesy?"

"Chum might think so, but I like it."

He clicked on the other dogs. Different voices.

"My brother recorded Fred for me, and Kat did Rat-Girl. I thought they turned out pretty good."

He agreed. In fact, he was blown away by her creativity. "How come you didn't show this to me earlier?"

She made a wobbly motion with her hand. "I guess I didn't trust my first effort. And I thought you'd think it was too off-the-wall. I mean, talking dogs? Come on." She shrugged.

He clicked on his image. Nothing happened. "You were going to ask me to record something, too."

"*Was* being the operative word. You're a recluse. I get that, now. I'm sorry I was so insensitive earlier."

He scooted the laptop between them. "Enthusiasm has its place, Rachel. Maybe I needed a kick in the butt to stir things up."

"A very attractive butt," she murmured softly. Not softly enough. He heard her. He wanted to finish what they'd started, but he couldn't. For her sake, more than his own.

Liar.

He stood. "Would you do me a favor and put some water on to boil? I need a cup of tea before I start working. This site is going to sell a lot more Dream-houses than I've got built."

"Does that mean I'm still employed?"

"Yes. I'll cut you a check when we get to the office. Do whatever you have to do to get this up and running on the Internet."

Her smile seemed to show her relief. Because he

was still her client or because he didn't follow up on her possible invitation? He didn't know. That was probably best.

For now.

He ignored the voice in his head. That voice had gotten him in trouble before. It made him want things he had no business wanting. Like a normal life.

AS SHE HEADED BACK into town a couple of hours later, Rachel congratulated herself on dodging not one near miss, but two. First, getting fired…and then getting laid. She wasn't sure how she felt about either.

Over tea, she and Rufus had firmed up the new site. He was adamant about keeping personal references to a minimum. He was perfectly okay with people wondering about his identity—even his gender, although she felt there were sufficient hints for people to figure out he was a man.

After a good half an hour of discussion, he'd agreed to let her use photos of the Black Hills on his site and okayed the mention of *Sentinel Passtime,* since having a popular television show filming in your area couldn't hurt from a PR prospective.

He also let her keep the dog's names. "They're more social than I am," he'd said with a rueful smile.

To her profound surprise, he'd been the one to suggest that she might consider writing a blog in one of the dogs' voices—possibly Chumley. "I, personally, don't see the point, but if you can show me stats on how many people seek out this sort of thing, I might let you make it a permanent part of the site. Of course, I'd pay you for this, in addition to your normal upkeep fees."

A good thing, she told herself. More money was

never bad, but writing a weekly blog would mean interacting probably one-on-one with the man she was finding more and more interesting. And attractive. And sexy.

She really hated to admit that. Seeing Rufus naked had given her imagination license to ponder things she had no business pondering.

Instead of heading to the quiet of her little bungalow, she turned toward the highway. The best way to avoid daydreams was to keep busy. And one way to do that would be to work on her brother's wedding plans.

First, she'd finish writing the code for Rufus's site and load it on her personal site to test so she could get a couple of unbiased reads from people whose opinion she trusted: Kat and Char.

"What do you think?" she asked Char two hours later.

Char was sitting at her computer behind the main desk at Native Arts, obviously doing her best to ignore Rachel's nervous pacing. She pushed back to swivel the chair about so they could see each other. "It's awesome. I love the talking dogs. You really are clever and creative. If I weren't going back to school, I'd hire you to completely revamp my Native Arts Web site." She frowned. "I simply can't afford a big overhaul right now."

"At least you have a legitimate reason for maintaining the status quo," Rachel answered. "With Rufus, I have to fight for each little change. You should have seen the look he gave me when I suggested setting up his own Facebook page. Equal parts terror and mortification."

Char's shoulders lifted and fell. "I've worked with a lot of artists over the years and some are very private people. Maybe they put so much of themselves into their work there's not enough left over to share with the general public."

"But Rufus is such a big guy," Rachel said, reveling in her private joke.

Char laughed. "Not what I meant, of course. My aunt used to say, 'The bigger they are, the deeper the hole they make when they hit the ground.'"

"Is this the aunt who has Alzheimer's? Too bad. She sounds like an interesting person. That's something you could blog about when you start doing a little social networking of your own." Char's expression rivaled Rufus's from earlier. So much so, Rachel couldn't help groaning. "What's with you people? Hasn't anyone in Sentinel Pass heard of the power of the Internet?"

"I know. I know. The TV people were all about Twitter the last time they filmed here, but change comes slowly to the mountains. I finally got video conferencing down with my aunt. One technical hurdle at a time."

Rachel rubbed her neck to ease some of her tension. If she were being honest she'd admit that coming to an agreement about how to market Rufus's work was only one small part of her problem. She was sexually attracted to the man. The more she tried not to picture what was under all those layers of really ugly plaid, the more she thought about what was under those really ugly layers.

"I think I'm on the verge of having a mental breakdown."

Char looked at her a good minute before replying. "You've been through a lot in a short time. Aren't moving and divorce number two and three on the list of emotional traumas?"

She had a point. Jack had encouraged Rachel to take some time off before plunging into a new business, but with the holidays approaching—the biggest retail time of the year—she hadn't felt she could afford to nurse her mental health.

Char snapped her fingers. "Not to mention you're planning your brother's wedding."

Rachel shook her head. "Oddly enough, the wedding is the least of my worries. Kat's so busy, she doesn't have time to micromanage anything, and Jack's so happy he agrees with everything I suggest. I love the power," she said, wiggling her eyebrows to show she was kidding.

"What does your mother say? She struck me as a bit of a control freak."

"Ya think?" Rachel joked. "She's golfing in Florida at the moment, but that doesn't keep her from adding her two cents about the wedding. Her text this morning said, 'No poinsettias. Too predictable.'"

Char's gaze shot to the four pots of gorgeous red flowers on the shelf. She and Rachel had already talked about using them on the altar. "Well, I'm no expert on motherhood, but I have been trying to take Libby's advice and listen more than I speak."

Rachel plucked a shriveled leaf off one of the plants. "Speaking of Libby. I got an e-mail from her last night. She and Cooper want me to design a Web site for a new charity they're setting up in his mother's and her grandmother's names. It's going to fund scholarships for single mothers and fathers returning to college. I'm really excited."

"That's awesome. Jenna told me she wanted to redo

the Mystery Spot's site before spring. I'm sure she'll be calling you, too. She and Shane are coming back for Christmas. It's gonna be hectic for a few weeks."

Rachel pressed her lips together in concentration. The gesture drew a question from Char. "What's wrong?"

"Nothing. The extra business will be great. But it's becoming increasingly obvious that I need an office. I can't keep using your computer. Libby's cottage is too small and it doesn't have DSL. Jack offered me space in his new office, but the county hasn't even approved his building plans. Apparently the attention from *Sentinel Passtime* started a mini land boom and the planning department has put a lot of items on hold until they do some environmental assessments. Do you know anyone with office space to rent?"

Char thought a moment. "What about Rufus? When Mac helped him build the studio, he said the second floor was intended for a future office. "

The thought had crossed Rachel's mind when Rufus gave her a tour of the place. Heat from the wood-burning stove passed through grates in the floor to make the upper landing cozy and comfortable. Plus, she'd have the added advantage of being present to shoot and upload photos of his new pieces on the spot. But could immediacy and convenience be enough to convince him to let her move in? Er, rent the space from him, she quickly amended.

"He made a point of telling me he didn't have DSL. He goes into town to use the computer at the community center."

Char shrugged. "By choice. He *could* install a modem. I bet the tower that provides service for the town is in line of sight of his place. But you probably know Rufus better than anybody. A year ago, if someone had told me he'd hire a Web designer to help him sell his art, I'd have called him a liar."

Rachel knew for a fact that a lot could change in twelve months. "It might work," she said, picturing where she'd put her desk and file cabinet. She could easily squeeze into the far corner without crowding his mostly unused desk area.

Char held up two thumbs, encouragingly. "Well, there you go. It can't hurt to ask." Char's grin turned mischievous. "What's the worst that could happen? You get snowed in and have to spend the night. Maybe there's more to the guy than any of us thought."

A whole lot more. Rachel bit on her lip to keep from blurting it out.

Char tossed up her hands. "Hey, I know he's not some gorgeous young calendar hunk, but based on how close you've gotten to him in such a short time, I'd say he might be sweet on you."

Sweet? Not the first word that came to mind when Rachel remembered his kiss. *Hot.* Much more apropos.

"I'm trying to set up a business here, remember? I'm not looking to date the guy." Before Char could say anything else, Rachel changed the subject. "When is book club again?"

"Libby's going to call everyone as soon as she and Cooper get home," Char said. "Is it me or is *A Thousand Splendid Suns* an odd choice for someone who is getting married in a few weeks?"

Libby had mentioned the same thing in her e-mail. "Kat told me she picked this book because it celebrates the power of the bond women share even in a society that devalues them."

Char pushed away from her computer and stood up. "Women power," she said, grinning. "Works for me. Plus, your future sister-in-law doesn't know how to take the easy road. She and Jack might never have gotten together if not for our book club."

Rachel smiled. Her brother had been pretty free with the details about his and Kat's unusual courtship. And Kat's friends had played *a* role, if not the defining one. Seeing her brother so happy had helped Rachel crawl out of her grief pit. She wanted that same joy and closeness some day, too. With someone she knew inside and out.

And Rufus horded secrets like a miser with gold bullion.

Which, she suddenly realized, might make him the perfect landlord. Not only was he a client—an automatic no-no from a business point of view—but also, the man was as transparent as a rock. It might have been easier keeping the boundary between them unfettered before she saw him naked, but she'd simply have to find a way to put that image out of her mind.

"You know what, Char? I think you might be right about renting office space from Rufus," she said. "It's not like I need a storefront for my operation. And he might need the money. He mentioned something about wanting all the profits to go to a cause near and dear to his heart. I didn't ask what it was or why, but every little bit helps, right?"

A part of her brain recognized the rationalizing for what it was, but another part knew that she came by her ability to compartmentalize honestly. Her mother had managed to carry on with her job at the bank, breaking the glass ceiling with steady perseverance and determination, even as her husband's reputation and standing in the community crumbled.

"So, let's talk flowers," she said. "I want to get the bouquets ordered before I head back up the hill to talk to Rufus. One major hurdle at a time."

CHAPTER EIGHT

To be absolutely certain she didn't arrive at Rufus's too early the next day, Rachel decided to run her idea of renting office space from Rufus by her brother.

She'd wound up spending several hours on the phone the day before with the florist and cake decorator. By the time she had the last detail ironed out, she hadn't wanted to risk the tricky drive to Rufus's at dusk.

Besides, what if he was *thinking* again? Soaking in his big copper tub. Wet and gorgeous.

"Hey, Rae," Jack said, greeting her at the door of his recently remodeled home. "Come and see the new Roman shades I'm hanging. Not bad for an amateur carpenter, huh?"

She wiped her feet carefully before following him inside. The place hardly resembled the photos she'd seen of it—bold paint choices, all new windows and a couple of walls had been removed to give it a more open feeling. Funny, she thought, how everyone still called it the Peterson place.

"Nice. Very nice. When are you getting your tree?"

He shrugged. "Don't know. Kat's mega busy. How are the wedding plans coming along? Everything okay?"

"Perfect. You're going to love the cake." She took a

breath, strangely hesitant to share her plan with Jack. She didn't know why. He certainly wasn't as judgmental as Mom.

"I'd like you to take a look at a rental agreement I put together. And my new business plan. If I'm going to be successful, Jack, I need space to create my designs and implement them."

Jack put down his bright yellow drill and pulled out a seat at the dining room table, motioning for her to sit, too. He read fast. "This looks great, Rachel. Rufus should jump at the chance to have an in-house Web designer. Who wouldn't?"

Rachel blew out a sigh of relief. "Thank you. You don't think six months is too ambitious, do you?"

She'd specified that her use of the rental space was only temporary. Six months tops. If all went as hoped, by summer she'd be in a position to purchase a house with enough space for a home office. Jack hadn't had any trouble finding an affordable home in Sentinel Pass, so she didn't expect to, either.

"Maybe. But you can always renegotiate. I see this as a win-win arrangement. But it's only office space, right? You're not moving in with the guy. Right?"

"Of course, not," she said, testily. "I barely know the man." *Even if I have seen him naked.* "He's my client, for heaven's sake. And a little…um…strange." Which, not surprisingly, she found a welcome change from her ex and his friends.

"The only problem I can see is that the guy clearly values his privacy. Does he have any real incentive to rent space to you? Financially, I mean?"

"He said he wants to sell as many Dreamhouses as

possible as quickly as possible. I'm taking that to mean he needs money, but I can't say for sure. He's not exactly an open book."

He looked at her for a few seconds, his eyebrows scrunched together. "You're not worried about being alone with him? I heard his place is pretty remote. What do you know about him?"

"Not much more than what you can read on his home page when it goes live," she said, honestly. "But Kat called him a gentle giant. And I know he's good to his dogs." *And he kisses like making out was a competitive sport and he was a gold medalist.*

He didn't look completely convinced. "Okay. Whatever you think. You're going to do what you want, anyway, but I appreciate the token asking of my opinion."

She stuck her tongue out at him.

He laughed and returned his attention to his shades.

"There's one other favor I need from you, Jackson."

"What's that?"

"Tell Mom we're not coming to Denver for Christmas."

His drill clattered to the table. "She doesn't really expect us… Surely you can't be serious… I'm getting married a few days after… Are you kidding?"

She laughed and patted his arm. "Of course she expects us. She's our mother. And I have to admit I feel a little guilty even suggesting we don't go home, but there's no way I can drive there and back with all the last-minute details and preparation."

"Well, I definitely can't go," Jack said, practically wringing his hands. "I promised the boys we'd open presents together on Christmas Eve. They're both spending Christmas day with their dads. This is important to them. And Kat's fried from classes and her practicum. I can't ask her to drive to Denver on Christmas morning then turn around and drive back to get married."

"That's what I figured. So…we have to make Mom come here. But where will she stay?"

Jack thought a moment. "Do you think she'd be mortally offended if I offered to find her a hotel room? She could stay here but she'd probably spend the whole time complaining about the smell of new paint."

"And aren't you and Kat and the boys planning to move in as soon as you get back from your honeymoon?" Jack and Kat were taking Jordie and Tag with them to Southern California for a week, then William, a family friend, would fly the boys home while Kat and Jack went on to Hawaii alone. Her sons would spend that week with each respective father.

He nodded. "Well…yes. But…"

"No buts. This is your home, Jack. Or will be very soon. Mom will simply have to roll with this, right?"

His expression said it all. Mom was no fan of change. Giving up her traditional Christmas celebration might come at a high price for all of them.

She gave her brother a quick hug and left. The more she thought about the upcoming holiday, the more she hoped Rufus would go for her plan. His remote, hilltop workshop was starting to look like a sanctuary.

Except for the drive, she thought half an hour later.

She flexed her fingers, which were stiff from gripping the steering wheel over the final few miles of rough road. She pulled in to the parking area that Rufus preferred she use then turned off the key and checked her watch. Eleven. Nice and late. Just the way Rufus

liked. Hopefully, he'd notice and appreciate her effort
to bend to his schedule.

The lack of energetic dogs racing out to greet her told
her their master was already at the workshop. The air
was brisk but not the deep cold they'd experienced for
a few days. The Black Hills weather was nothing if not
unpredictable.

"Hey," Rufus said, meeting her at the door.

"Hi. How's it going?" she asked, a bit breathless
from her walk…and anticipation of their meeting.

He stepped aside to let her in. "Fine."

"Good." She stomped off what little snow was stuck
to her boots. Stalling. An awkward silence ballooned
between them, until Rachel blurted, "Rufus, I need an
office, and I want to rent the second floor of your
workshop. Here's my proposition."

While he helped her out of her jacket, she unzipped
her briefcase and pulled out the sheet of paper she'd
shown Jack. He read it through then looked at her
targeted space. "How much?"

She blinked. That was so not the answer she'd been
expecting. "Um. Well, I put together a business plan,
too. I need to turn a profit, and that means keeping my
overhead low while I'm getting started. Of course, I
don't expect you to open up your space to me for free."
She swallowed. "Four hundred dollars a month?"

"You're going to want a telephone, aren't you? And
Internet hookup."

She gulped. "Yes. Char said that wouldn't be a
problem, but I'd be happy to check on what satellite
service might involve. I could pay that separately."

His brow was crinkled and his lips were smushed

together in a tight line. "I looked into it a while back. Thought I might be able to learn HTML or whatever it's called on my own."

"And you decided...?"

"I'd be better off trying to learn Sanskrit." He shook his head. "I've been mulling over what you said and if these things start selling, I'm definitely going to need someone to keep track of sales and ship them off. I can't do that *and* spend fifteen hours a day building Dreamhouses. It's not humanly possible."

She wondered if the last was a reference to her claim he was part yeti. "I agree. And I'm perfectly happy getting the sales-and-distribution end of this business up and running and help train someone to take over." That brought another frown. She understood how a self-designated hermit might not welcome the concept of employees, but if his sales did as well as she expected, he would need help. At some point. For now, she needed him to need her.

She pointed to the open area above his workshop. "There's plenty of room for my office and a distribution center," she told him, clearly seeing the configuration. "My desk and filing cabinets would fit nicely in the far corner by the window—better ventilation and out of your way. Your printer is excellent and your computer can easily handle orders. So, we leave your existing desk where it is and move the U-shape table you have downstairs to handle packing and shipping."

He stared at where she was pointing, but she was certain the image didn't jump out at him as it did to her.

"I know it sounds like a big change, but I promise you everything will meld together nicely. And, this way, you'll have more control than if you hired a company off-site to process your orders."

She refrained from getting into the whole PayPal and online credit card sale aspect. She couldn't picture him handling this side of the business himself. Like the man said, there was only so much a body could humanly do.

"How 'bout we make this a trade? As long as I'm handling the accounting, sales and distribution aspect, my hours will be applied to my rent? When you're ready to hire someone else to do that or I need more time to devote to my business, we reassess where we're at—rent-wise."

Rufus's stomach cramped at the thought of bringing in another person to work in his previously private, sacrosanct space. What she was proposing was by far the lesser of several evils. He was comfortable with her... well, as much as he could be given the fact he desired her.

"Okay."

"Okay? Really? Just like that? Don't you want to haggle about the price or my hourly rate? Nothing?"

He shook his head. He'd been up much of the night wondering if it was too late to back out of his commitment to Stephen's House. He couldn't. He knew that. The charity was counting on him, as they had from the beginning. As they had every right to since the idea of Stephen's House was his.

"No."

She opened her mouth and closed it. A second later, she crossed her arms and said, "That was too easy. You're a recluse. You don't divvy up your personal space without a fight. What gives? Come on. Tell me."

Could he? His mind balked, but a part of him knew

this time was coming. Maybe from the moment they kissed. She'd gotten under his skin and broken through the invisible parameter he'd worked so hard to keep in place. The tricky part was explaining his involvement in the charity without sounding like he was bragging. That was definitely not the case.

"All the money I make is going to a charity I helped start." At the time, he'd been rolling in dough. He'd made his initial donation using his professional name and had called in as many favors as possible from people in the business to set up significant seed money.

"What kind of charity?"

"It's called Stephen's House. It's in Mitchell. A couple of hundred miles east of here. The board of directors has raised several million dollars to build a guest residence for families of patients who are hospitalized for long periods of time. Comas. Accidents. Chronic illnesses. That sort of thing."

After Rufus's initial fund-raising effort, the dedicated volunteers and citizens of Mitchell continued to drive the project with unflagging support. The same generosity of spirit they'd shown when his brother was hospitalized.

"Wow. That's wonderful." She hesitated a moment then asked, "Do you mind telling me why you're involved? It's none of my business. I just—"

"My mother had to drive seventy miles every day to stay with my brother, Stephen, during the four months he was in a coma." Had there been a place like Stephen's House for Mom and Dad to stay in during that time, things might have turned out differently. Stephen would still be gone, but his parents might have pulled together throughout the tragedy, instead of pulling apart. Rufus might not have carried the deep emotional scars that changed his life forever.

She cleared the distance between them and placed a hand on his arm. "I can't imagine how difficult that must have been. Did he pull through?"

"No." He didn't want to talk about Stephen. That was too personal. So, he told her about the charity. His small balm to ease his guilt. "We're only a few months away from opening. It's a twenty-room house with a kitchen and a yard for younger siblings. But without money, there won't be any beds, TVs, chairs, tables…"

She nodded. "I get the picture. You need to keep your overhead low and your profits high. We can do this."

She made it sound easy.

"My moving in will work to your advantage. Think how timely it will be when you finish a new piece," she told him, her enthusiasm unwavering despite his silence. "I can upload the photo almost instantaneously."

"*If* my Dreamhouses sell." It was tempting to be swept up in her enthusiasm and optimism, but he knew better than anyone that mere wishing didn't make something come true.

She brushed aside his doubt. "They will. In fact, let me get settled a bit then we'll run through the finalized version of the prototype we discussed. Once I have your approval, I'll clean up all the code and make the site go live when I get into town. Tomorrow morning at the latest."

Go live. The irony didn't escape him.

He started toward the storage area. "I'll move the table upstairs for you."

She let out a little peep. "Just like that. That was easy. Is there a hitch?"

Yes. He'd been trying to think of a way—short of flat-out telling her—to keep her from stopping by his house every morning. "There's a small refrigerator in the closet. I haven't used it in a long time, but I think it works." It had chilled many a bottle of Dom Pérignon when it was in his dressing room. "You can bring a microwave or hot plate if you want."

She tilted her chin in a way he was beginning to know meant she got his point. "You don't want me up at the house anymore."

Smart and sexy. After all, she was the one who called what happened between them a *Titanic* disaster. The less contact they had together outside of work the better. "I'll be working most of the time," he said. A token excuse but one that sounded better than "I can't walk into my bedroom now without picturing you there."

"Of course," she murmured. "Me, too."

There was more to say but he didn't have the heart for it. He'd received a letter from an attorney representing a collective of investors like him who had lost mega bundles. He supported the group's effort but the initial retainer wasn't cheap and the chance of recouping anything substantial would be years and years down the road. All that was left to him at this point was this slim hope that Rachel knew what she was talking about, that her gift for design and knowledge of that vast, unnerving universe called the Internet would serve him well enough to keep his dream alive.

Maybe he'd build himself a Dreamhouse and write "Furnish Stephen's House" on a piece of paper to tuck into the hidey-hole. It might not be his only dream, but it was the most important. And the least selfish.

"Stephen would have been twice the man you are, Rob. Stevie was thoughtful and giving every day of his life. All you've ever done is take, son," his father had said the night Stephen died.

Rufus proceeded to spend his twenties making his father's condemnation a self-fulfilling prophecy. His thirties bargaining with God for a second chance. And, given that second chance, he'd made a vow to do something good. He was finally within a few feet of the peace-of-mind finish line. He wouldn't give in to any personal distractions no matter how alive they—*she*—made him feel. To fall for Rachel would prove his father was right.

CHAPTER NINE

RACHEL LIKED TO THINK she wasn't the kind of person who went around saying "I told you so," but she was feeling pretty smug. Today was Friday. They'd agreed on the rough design and format for Rufus's site on Wednesday and she made it live the following morning. In less than twenty-four hours, they'd recorded twelve purchases.

And considering the price she and Rufus had agreed on, this was pretty significant, she thought, barely able to keep from dancing as she watched raptly as the printer spit out the list of mailing labels.

"Paid in full," she said a few moments later, waving the paper in front of Rufus's nose. As usual, he was perched on his stool, intently assembling a new Dreamhouse. "Three to Colorado. One to New Hampshire. Two to Texas," she bragged. "How cool is that?"

He pushed his clear goggles to the top of his head and removed his earplugs. "You're dying to say, 'I told you so,' aren't you?" he asked, spinning to face her.

"Yes. But I'm far too mature. I'll settle for doing a happy dance." To prove it, she broke into a silly, silent soft-shoe that made him chuckle.

"Good thing I've been stockpiling these." He looked at the clock that had appeared on the wall that morning.

"Are you going to try to ship them today? I'll help you carry the boxes up to the house for Clive."

She'd had her first face-to-face with the letter carrier yesterday. "Yes. Clive. I had no idea men could be such big gossips."

Rufus's presence might have made the transaction go more smoothly, since quite a few of Clive's probing questions had been about Rufus and his new business.

Rufus didn't comment, but he did stand, forcing her to take a step back. They'd both been extra careful to keep their contact strictly professional.

"Any help would be great," she said, heading toward the area where Rufus stored his finished products. "A quick turnaround will impress the buyers and foster potential referrals. With any luck, they'll chat us up to their friends."

"On Facebook?"

She'd shown him a couple of her social networking sites yesterday, after she'd gotten the DSL connected. "Maybe. Or Twitter."

He didn't say anything. She got the impression the jury was still out on whether he considered this connection to the outer world a good thing or bad.

"Which ones are going out?" he asked.

Metal shelves had been erected against three walls with two large tables in the center of the room. The place was neat, but his method of organization escaped her completely. Instead of numbering each unit, as she'd suggested, he named them. Sunshine was on the left, one shelf above Air. While he could operate on memory, she was forced to zigzag around like a disoriented bee collecting pollen. Body contact was almost impossible to avoid.

"Oomph," Rufus grunted when his shoulder grazed hers.

"Should we take turns next time?"

She was kidding but he seemed serious when he muttered, "Good idea."

Once all six were assembled, he wrapped his arms around four and walked to the door. He waited for her to grab the other two. She carried her load quite effortlessly, but she noticed he was showing signs of exertion by the time they reached the second floor.

"You haven't had time to look in to my dumbwaiter idea, have you?" he said, carefully setting his load on the shipping desk. They'd had this conversation earlier when discussing logistics. The storage area was convenient for him but too small a space to store peripheral necessities such as boxes, packing peanuts and his printer.

"I checked several sites. The new ones aren't cheap, but I'll keep looking. Even wholesale, they'll probably run a couple of grand."

"That might be worthwhile if I planned on making a career of this," he said, his tone pensive.

She grabbed one of the flattened boxes she'd picked up at the post office the day before and popped it open. One size, one rate. "What do you mean?"

"I told you. The money I make from these goes to Stephen's House. Once it's up and running…" He shrugged. "Who knows what will happen after that?"

Yeah, yeah, she understood his present needs. Noble and selfless, she got that. But surely that didn't mean this was a one-shot deal. She couldn't fathom putting so much time and effort into building a company then simply letting it go. "So…you see yourself getting bored with Dreamhouses and maybe branching out? No pun intended."

Her smile faltered when he turned to face her. "You're young and ambitious. You wouldn't understand."

That stung. When her father was unjustly accused of molesting a young client, her mother would send Rachel to bed so she could call Jack, who was in college, and tell him all the details Mom deemed inappropriate for Rachel to hear. "You wouldn't understand, dear," Mom had always said.

But Rachel did understand. Because she'd sneak down the hall to eavesdrop. That's how she learned about the lawsuit. Later, her snooping revealed her father's cancer, and, after a certain point, she overheard him tell her mother about his decision to decline treatment.

She crossed her arms and glared at him. "Yeah, right. I'm practically a child. A college-graduate, self-employed, divorced kid. I might lack experience in certain matters, but don't tell me I lack empathy. I'm not your partner in this business, but I do have a certain vested interest given the amount of time I've spent working on selling you. The least you can do is keep me abreast of your long-term strategy. Or lack of one."

He stretched his neck like a man who had been hunched over a workbench too long. "I told you. I have a goal, not a plan." He held up his hands. She noticed for the first time a couple of adhesive bandages. "Physically, I don't know how long I'll be able to keep it up."

She fought an irrational desire to kiss his ouchies. A motherly thing to do and she was not the motherly type. Instead of comforting him, she tried to think logically. "You could hire someone to help you. A protégé. All the great masters had them. He or she could assemble the base unit and you could add that special Rufus Miller touch."

His left eyebrow cocked in a way she'd come to know meant bemusement. "And where would I find such a person?"

"I don't know, but I could ask Char. She works with lots of artists. Or maybe the local colleges have art departments that offer internships."

His lips pulled to one side, confirming once again in her mind how much better he'd look without facial hair.

An idea that had been dancing around in her mind all morning suddenly launched itself on to her tongue. "You know…if money is an issue, and I certainly do get that it is, I might have a way to add to your coffers." She wouldn't have considered the idea if not for the e-mail she received the night before from Trevor. Her ex wanted to buy "his" Porsche back from her, and he was willing to pay top dollar. Apparently he'd won a couple of big tournaments recently and was feeling flush. That was okay with her. In fact, giving it back felt rather liberating, although she couldn't say exactly why.

"Like what?" Rufus asked.

"I need a date to my brother's wedding and I'd be willing to pay for an escort." She held up her hand. "I know what you're thinking. How could anybody be so desperate they'd pay good money for fake companionship? Well, real companionship, but fake fraternity."

Was that the right word? Probably not, but she hadn't had time to prepare a well-thought out argument.

"What's the answer?"

"Pardon?"

"How could you be so desperate?"

"Oh. One word. Mom. She loves me but she's constantly trying to fix me. Not fix me up, although finding the right mate for me is never far from her mind. Mostly, she doesn't think I'm capable of navigating a proper course to personal fulfillment without the steady hand of a man at the helm."

She laughed at his look of horror. She hurried to reassure him. "I love her. Really. I do. She wants the best for me. We simply don't agree what that is. And if I come to the wedding with a date, your presence would take the focus off the fact that I'm alone, and switch it to how absolutely wrong you are for me."

She kept her tone light, but she was serious.

She fully expected him to say no. So when he asked, "How much?" she nearly fell over.

"Good question. What's the going rate for a date these days? I don't want to insult you. How 'bout two hundred dollars?" She was getting a lot more for the Porsche than she'd hoped, she could afford to waste a little bit.

"Make it five and I'll go to the party, too."

The party was Libby and Cooper's holiday bash. Obviously, he'd overheard her babbling about it in an online interface she'd had with Char.

Five hundred dollars. He'd made it clear the money he was working so hard to procure was going toward a good cause, not to put new tires on his old truck. "Okay. It's a deal. On one condition."

He waited, eyes narrowed.

"You shave."

His lips pursed again. Such nice, masculine lips. She wished kissing him wasn't on her "Threat Level: Orange" list of no-nos.

"Deal. On one condition." He looked serious. "No pictures of me. Zero. Zip. Nada."

She couldn't imagine why that was so important but she certainly didn't plan to argue. "I can live with that. Libby assured me she's only invited family and close friends. And Kat and Jack aren't famous so there won't be any paparazzi at the wedding."

Her mother would be aghast at Rachel's choice of date, beard or no beard, but Rachel couldn't wait to see Rufus's face sans whiskers. In fact, she was a little giddy imagining how he'd look.

"So," she said, "let's get this show on the road. I don't want to miss Clive. Maybe you should let the dogs out so they can tree him."

Rufus laughed for real. "He hasn't gotten out of his truck without me present since Rat-Girl moved in."

"I love that dog. Did you know she's started napping on my toes when I'm sitting at the computer? Warm and sweet. I'm really touched."

He looked at her feet. When his gaze made the return trip, it seemed to slow and study her with a certain wistfulness or longing. He caught her watching, though, and quickly reached for a packing box. Maybe he had his own Threat Levels going on.

Half an hour later, Rufus watched as Rachel charmed the often brusque and grouchy letter carrier with an ease Rufus had never possessed—even when he was at the top of his popularity and people competed to please him.

He wasn't sure why he'd agreed to Rachel's request to be an escort. Probably something to do with the way she'd characterized her mother. He'd heard a hint of ache beneath her bravado and understood all too well. Rufus had had someone like that in his life for a time— by choice, not by birth, which probably made him some kind of masochist.

Marianne Diminici, his ex-agent, was known as The Great White in Gucci. She'd spelled out her business philosophy from the day he signed with her. "Never forget that handsome men are everywhere. The day you stop making me money is the day I drop you."

She'd made good on that promise while Rufus was still in the hospital recovering from surgery. She'd sent him flowers, a very large check and a short note.

It was good while it lasted.
M.

Looking at Rachel, he wondered what his life would have been like if he'd gone the normal route: college, marriage, kids and career. Fame and fortune didn't guarantee happiness. That much he knew for certain.

"A good day all around, wouldn't you say?" she said, rejoining him with a satisfied smile on her face as Clive's truck pulled out of the driveway.

He agreed but didn't say so. "When's the party?"

Her slight hesitation made him think she might be regretting their bargain. "Tomorrow night. Sixish. Not much time, huh? Do you…need anything?" The pink in her cheeks from the chilly breeze turned a slightly deeper shade. "Like clothes? This isn't black tie or anything, but my dress is sorta glitzy. I wouldn't want you to feel out of place."

She was beautiful when she was flustered. She had

no way of knowing he had an entire walk-in closet filled with high-end designer clothes, including shoes that cost more than the entire shipment that just left.

She clapped her hands to her face. "Oh, pooh. Don't listen to me. Wear whatever you like. And you don't have to shave if you don't want to. Really. That was rude and insensitive on my part. I must have been channeling Mom. I'm thankful you agreed to go with me."

Rufus ran his fingers over his beard. He hadn't intentionally set out to create a new persona when he moved here, but as his hair grew back after his chemo treatments, he'd found comfort in the normalcy it provided. Long hair hid his scars; a beard made him look less gaunt after the considerable weight loss. Now, both were conveniences that kept people at bay. Everyone except Rachel.

"I'll shave."

She still looked worried. "My mother tends to put a lot of stock in appearances, but I don't. At least, that's what I'd like to believe. So, please, don't change a single thing about yourself for my sake." She reached out and touched his arm. "And I promise to do my best not to let her hurt your feelings."

That made him smile. She was worried about him. When was the last time someone worried about how he felt? He couldn't remember.

"I lived in New York. Thick skin comes with the territory."

Her relief was obvious, but he could tell she still had reservations. He could have cited examples of the reviews he'd received over the years:

"His nose is too large."

"His ears are too small."

"His ass is great but there's a tiny bit of muscle bulk on his upper thigh I'd like him to lose. By Friday."

The last edict had been issued by an art director on a Wednesday. Rufus had laughed. Marianne had actually called around to see if there was such a thing as instant liposuction of muscle.

Rachel shifted from side to side, drawing his attention to the fact that she wasn't dressed in five layers of wool, as he was. She wore black pants and boots, but she'd left her jacket in the shop. Her Nordic design sweater had nice lines but didn't look very warm.

"Cup of tea?" he asked, his voice catching slightly.

She hadn't been inside the main house since that accidental-naked-bathtub moment.

Her gaze shot toward the house. "Oh. Uh…no, thanks. I think I'll head into Rapid. A few last-minute gifts for my future nephews."

Kat's sons. Rufus had seen them from a distance. They looked like nice kids. The younger one reminded him of his brother.

He walked beside her as they hurried toward the shop. Curious, he asked, "What are you buying them?"

"Mother got them a Wii. Do you know what that is?"

He nodded, amused rather than put out that she assumed he was commercially illiterate.

"I told her I'd pick up a couple of games. I've been debating about Guitar Hero. It looks fun, but they might be a little young. I don't know."

"Boys like to think they're old enough for something even if they're not. I promise you that."

She laughed. "So I should get it?"

He nodded.

"Okay. But if Kat complains, I'm blaming you."

To his surprise, Rufus found he didn't mind. In fact, it felt good to be part of something. Even something as small as giving the wrong advice for a Christmas present.

Had he been missing that kind of connection for a while or had meeting Rachel been the catalyst for change? He didn't know, but he did know that he was looking forward to this party.

CHAPTER TEN

THE MUSIC WASN'T traditional Christmas songs. It was bluegrass. Supplied by a live band. Four talented young musicians who played banjo, bass, cello and, of all things, a glockenspiel. Rachel was mesmerized. So much so, she almost forgot that her date was late.

"I didn't know there was going to be a band," Rachel said to Char, standing beside her.

"A gift from Cooper. Libby's been a fan of these guys ever since she heard them a few years ago at a music fest in Spearfish. They're from Boston. Aren't they awesome?"

Rachel agreed. The lead singer's voice was lovely and plaintive. The lyrics seemed especially poignant. Or maybe it was the emotional nature of the holiday season. So many chances for disappointment and regret.

She still harbored some regret about pressuring Rufus to come to this party as her date. Given twenty-eight hours of hindsight, she was certain she'd come off as both insensitive and shallow. *Please be my date. But, first, change everything about yourself because I have to try to make my mother believe the impossible—that I'm happy.* The fact that her mother wouldn't believe Rachel could be happy without a man opened up a dialogue Rachel had no intention of pursuing.

"Your date is late," Char observed.

"So is yours."

Char's smile didn't seem the least bit bothered. "Eli is at Native Arts getting ready. He's coming as Lakota Santa Claus. Instead of dropping off presents, he's picking up all the gifts everyone brought to distribute to needy kids on the reservation. Cool, huh?"

Rachel looked at the huge pile of festively wrapped gifts stacked beside the Christmas tree. She'd bought two handmade dolls from Char's shop and two remote controlled trucks that Jordie and Tag swore were the best. Shopping for the giveaway gifts had been almost as much fun as shopping for Kat's sons. "Awesome. Are you going with him?"

Char nodded. "I've got my elf hat in my purse." Her smile fell slightly. "It was tough putting Damien on the plane this morning. I wanted him to be here so everyone could meet him, but we had to strike some sort of compromise so he could be with his other mother and siblings."

Rachel gave her friend a quick hug. "I really admire the way you put Damien's feelings first, Char. And he's going to be here for the wedding, right?"

Char's smile returned with a joy that Rachel envied. She was looking forward to the wedding but not with the same kind of intensity. This was a sort of make-or-break moment for her. She needed to prove to herself—and her toughest critic—that she could accomplish whatever she set out to do.

A server with a small silver tray approached them. "Grilled shrimp with Hawaiian dipping sauce?"

Rachel laughed. "That's the most nontraditional holiday fare I've ever seen. Sure. Give me one." She shifted her flute of champagne to her left hand and stabbed a mouthwatering-looking shrimp with a red toothpick.

"Mmm," she said, chewing. "Good. Really good. We might want to serve these at the wed—" Her train of thought left her the moment she spotted Libby's brother, Mac, opening the door for the newest arrival.

A *Sentinel Passtime* cast member, she assumed, swallowing a sigh of disappointment along with her shrimp. The tall, well-built stranger was definitely not from around here. As he handed Mac his expensive-looking black wool coat, she noticed his suit. A gray so dark it could almost be classified as black. It hugged his wide shoulders as if it had been sewn for him.

She was about to ask Char if she thought the man might be wearing Armani, but decided that sounded ridiculously shallow. Instead, she polished off the remainder of her shrimp.

Chewing, she continued to study the new arrival. There was something commanding in the man's look, his manner, his gaze. Which he turned on her, almost as though he'd been looking for her.

"Oh," she inhaled in surprise and all too sudden comprehension, remembering too late her mouth was full of half-masticated shrimp.

Char gave Rachel a few whacks on the back. "I suppose choking is one way to catch a man's attention," she joked. "Who is that guy? Do you know him? He looks like an actor but I don't remember seeing anyone that handsome around." She made a face of pure horror. "Wait. What am I saying? Eli's that handsome and then some. And if you tell him I was drooling over a gorgeous stranger, I will make sure Santa leaves a lump of coal in your stocking."

"He's not a stranger," Rachel whispered, after swallowing with considerable difficulty. "That's my date."

"Your date? I thought you were waiting for Rufus?" Char asked, puzzled.

"I am." Rachel nodded, trying to act cool, despite the heat flushing through her every corpuscle.

She watched the conflicting emotions of bafflement and incredulity play across her friend's face. "That's Rufus Miller?"

The band chose that moment to take a break and normal chatter went mute as people turned to watch Rufus walk across the room. His gaze left Rachel's long enough to bow politely to Char. "Happy holidays, and congratulations on your recent engagement. Rachel told me the good news."

Char got over her obvious shock quite quickly. "Thank you, Rufus. I understand congratulations are in order for you, too. Rachel told me your site has had a gazillion hits and you're selling Dreamhouses like crazy."

"Thanks to Rachel." He looked at Rachel again with the most inside-out, depths-of-your-soul look she'd ever received. She had no idea what to say but she had to say something.

"You cut your hair. You didn't have to. I told you not to. I feel like such a jerk. You must hate me."

He didn't say anything for a minute then he smiled. His grin of amusement that did crazy things to her equanimity. "It was time. The hairdresser said my split ends had split ends of their own."

She couldn't stop herself. She reached up and touched his bare jaw. "And you shaved. I thought maybe the beard was hiding something. Like a weak chin, but you're handsome, Rufus. Really, surreally handsome."

The twinkle in his eyes seemed to imply that the joke was on her. Was she simply slow to see something everyone else had always known? A flash of pique made her add, "Why am I always the last to know these things?"

Before he could answer, her brother grabbed her arm. "Hey, Rae, I need you a sec…whoa. Hold on. Rufus?" Jack's mouth dropped open far enough to see his perfect orthodontia. "Holy cripes. Man, you clean up good. Who'd have known?"

Jack had met Rufus formally the week before when he helped Rachel move into her new office space. His surprise quelled a bit of Rachel's anger, but she still felt unsettled. Why did a gorgeous, healthy, vital young man—shaving his beard had taken a good twenty years off his overall appearance—bury his beauty beneath layers of plaid? She didn't get it. And she was half-afraid to hear the answer.

"Your sister asked me come as her date. I figured that meant a haircut was in order."

"Well, you look great." Jack's eyes narrowed slightly. "And kinda familiar. Have we met? Before Sentinel Pass, I mean." He tossed up his hands. "Oh, hell, how's that possible, right? I'll stop babbling now. Can I get you something to drink?"

Rachel started to say that he didn't drink, but Rufus answered first. "Red wine."

"Red it is. Rachel? A refill?"

She shook her head. "Later. Thanks. What did you need me for?"

Jack waved off the question. "Mom was looking for you, but she'll find you sooner or later. Especially once she hears you brought a date." He grinned broadly. "This

is gonna be good. Finally, a break from the scrutiny."
He paused to shake Rufus's hand. "Thanks, man. You're
a lifesaver. I mean it."

Rufus had a feeling he knew what Rachel's brother
meant by the last comment. The more he heard about
Jack and Rachel's mother, the less he liked her. But he
reminded himself not to jump to conclusions.

"I didn't think you drank," Rachel said softly.

He hadn't planned on it, but the moment the door
closed behind him, he'd felt a familiar fluttery sensation
in the pit of his stomach. Nerves. Until he spotted Rachel.

Tall, willowy, self-possessed. Her glitzy red cocktail
dress clung to her every curve. She was gorgeous. But
more important, she was real. A beautiful security blanket
for an insecure man who traditionally hid his insecurities
behind an oversize ego and too much booze and drugs.

He could tell his new look surprised her. Shock and
awe, Marianne would have said. And for some reason,
she seemed a bit peeved. As if he'd pulled some elaborate hoax on her.

He leaned close enough to keep the conversation
private. "Don't forget. You've seen me naked."

Her beautifully made-up eyes widened. She surprised him by not having a quick comeback. Maybe she
wasn't as perceptive as he'd thought. That was disap-
pointing, and meant he was in for a long evening.

"So," he said, trying to recall some of his old con-
versational tricks from back in the day, "who are all
these people? I recognize a few from town, but—"

"The three men by the refreshment table talking to
Jack are Jenna's fiancé, Shane, Libby's brother, Mac,
and Morgan's agent, William."

Rufus didn't believe in stereotyping people, but early in his career he'd learned a vital lesson: read people or be eaten alive. The men she pointed out seemed relaxed, confident and successful. They were comfortable in their skin. He was envious. And conflicted. He'd actually enjoyed shaving that morning. Getting a haircut had brought back a wealth of memories—more good than bad. Dressing in clothes from his old life had felt surprisingly exciting.

His dogs had sniffed around him at length. Rat-Girl had acted as if he'd killed her old master and buried the body somewhere. Maybe he had.

Lifting up slightly on the toes of her four-inch patent leather pumps, she said, "Kat's boys are around here somewhere." She smiled and nodded. "There. By the tree. And Megan is with them. See that darling little girl in the fancy dress? The woman beside her is Mac's fiancé, Morgana Carlyle. She goes by Morgan when she's around friends. And there's Libby. Can't miss her."

Rufus knew Libby. She'd been kind to him when he first moved to Sentinel Pass and he was pleased to see her looking so happy…and healthily pregnant. She acknowledged him with a bright, welcoming smile.

He half tuned out the rest of Rachel's play-by-play of attendees. He meant to listen, but over the past few years he'd learned to listen to senses other than hearing, and he felt a powerful force headed their way even before the bodies around them parted for the older woman in four-inch heels and a high-neck black wool dress with a dramatic *V* of bright gold buttons.

"Here you go," Jack said, thrusting a wineglass in his hand. "Gotta dash. The boys need me."

Rufus knew a fake excuse when he heard one. Jack's true goal was to stay under the radar of the woman bearing down on them. Rachel had her back to the crowd, but Rufus saw her jolt to attention the instant the woman said, "Rachel, I've been looking all over for you."

Rachel's eyes were wide, but Rufus couldn't read what she was thinking. Her lips pulled to one side for a moment, but the rueful gesture was replaced almost instantly by a smile as she turned around. "Hi, Mom. I was hoping you'd find me so I could introduce you to my date, Rufus Miller. Rufus, this is my mother, Rosaline Treadwell."

His gut told him everything he needed to know even before he touched the woman's hand. Powerful, controlling and, at the moment, unhappy. "Ma'am," he said, bending slightly. He didn't bother laying on the charm. She'd surely see right through him.

"You're Rachel's one and only client, aren't you? I've warned her about mixing business and pleasure."

Rachel made a coughing sound. "Really? Was that before or after you introduced me to Trevor? Your bank's hired spokesperson."

"You weren't doing business with him, dear. I was."

Rachel might have said more but a robust flurry of bell ringing suddenly filled the air. "Could I have everyone's attention a moment?" Libby said from her perch on a low stool. Her husband, Cooper Lindstrom, the blond, easily recognizable television star, hovered nearby, a fretful look on his classically handsome face. "Coop and I wanted to thank you all for coming on such short notice. When Gran was alive, the holidays were always jam-packed with parties and good friends. Thanks for helping me to keep her tradition alive."

Everyone clapped, except Rufus and Rachel's mother.

"Also, my heartfelt thanks to the band, Crooked Still, for stopping off in the Hills on their way home for the holidays. What a fabulous present from my amazing husband." She planted a kiss on Cooper's lips, then added, "Speaking of gifts, thank you all for bringing these fabulous gifts for the toy drive. Santa should be here any minute to take them away and put them in the hands of children who will love them."

After another round of applause died down, she pointed to the gaily lit tree a few feet away. "We also thank you from the bottom of our hearts for your amazingly generous donations to the causes of your heart."

Cooper leaned over and snatched an envelope from a branch to hand her. "Each one of these will help someone somewhe—" Her emotions got the better of her and she reached in the pocket of her maternity sweater for a tissue.

Cooper pulled her close and finished her sentence. "Someone somewhere will appreciate your generosity so very much. This envelope alone holds a check for a thousand dollars. We know how tight the economy is and we didn't expect to see this kind of giving."

Rufus's heart rate sped up the instant he recognized his handwriting and the name on the envelope. But, thankfully, Cooper kept his promise to leave Rufus's name out of any public acknowledgment.

"It was probably from Shane," Rachel's mother said. "I think he's rich. What's unusual is not taking credit for the gift. I don't understand anonymous donations."

"Whoever it is has his or her reasons, Mom." Rachel looked at Rufus when she said this, as if guessing that the check might belong to him.

Rufus could have sent his check off to Stephen's House without going through the Lindstroms' gifting tree, but the day he overheard Rachel discussing the charitable project with Char, he'd changed his plan. Why? To impress Rachel's friends? If that were the case, then why insist on anonymity? He didn't have an answer.

"Do you speak?" her mother asked him bluntly.

He gave her his full attention. He could see where Rachel got her beauty, but Rachel's features were softer and more approachable. "On occasion."

"What sort of occasion? If not at a party like this, why bother coming?"

"I twisted his arm, Mother. So you wouldn't feel sorry for me and try to fix me up."

Rufus offered his arm to Rachel. "And you're right, Mrs. Treadwell. I've been remiss in my socializing. If you'll excuse us, I should greet our host and hostess."

Rachel looked surprised by the gesture, but she didn't hesitate to accept. Rufus's sixth sense told him her mother didn't like him. Not one bit. And that actually made him quite happy. The old Rufus would have automatically sought to change her opinion. Thank God he wasn't that person any longer.

RACHEL STOOD IN THE DOORWAY of the kitchen and sipped her glass of water as she watched Rufus charm his miniature audience. He'd removed his tie an hour or so earlier and opened his pristine white shirt collar a few buttons. She didn't understand why she found that glimpse of flesh so provocative, but she did. So much so, in fact, she'd made up an excuse about needing a drink of water simply to give herself some breathing space.

"Your date seems to like children" a voice observed. Rachel started. Her mom-radar must have malfunctioned.

"They seem to like him, too," Rachel returned cautiously, wondering where this conversation would lead. Nowhere good, she was sure.

"I wonder why that is?" Mom said. "Perhaps because he's a bit…simple."

Rachel put the glass to her mouth and forced herself to drink. It was that or scream. And she couldn't scream because her father never would have allowed it. The man worshipped his wife and let her get away with all sorts of small cruelties.

"You're basing your judgment on what? A two-second conversation?"

"I asked around. People who drop out of society, as he did, usually do so for a reason, Rachel. Do you know what that reason is?"

No. "He's my client, Mom. I'm on a need-to-know basis, and his personal life is something I don't need to know—as long as he pays my bill. I invited him tonight because I thought his business would benefit from the local exposure."

Rachel was pleased by how logical and composed she sounded. For a minute, she thought her mother bought it.

Mom shook her perfectly coifed head. "Don't kid yourself, Rachel. You're attracted to him. And, with good reason. He's quite handsome. But I thought you told me you'd learned your lesson where handsome men were concerned. I believe your exact words included *hook nose* and *bald.*"

Rachel set her glass on an antique sideboard then crossed her arms. "I may have said something to that effect, but, Mother, surely you're not labeling all handsome men as cheating scoundrels who can't keep their dicks in their pants. I could point out half a dozen hunks in this room—including your son—and each one is a faithful, trustworthy and decent human being who loves his wife and knows how to honor his marriage vows."

"There's no reason to be crude, Rachel. All I'm saying is you need to look beyond the superficial. You have a tendency to jump in to everything with both feet. In a relationship, by the time you discover how shallow the man is, something's broken."

Rachel gave her mother credit for creating an apropos metaphor. She'd been fighting an attraction toward this man since that first day. But what did she know about him? She hadn't known he was drop-dead gorgeous. Or good with kids. Or even that he owned a suit.

"There you are," a deep voice said, taking both women by surprise. Rufus leaned in and brushed a quick, micro-kiss on Rachel's lips. "Sorry. Those kids are great. Jordie reminds me of my little brother when he was that age."

Rachel had to fight to keep from touching the spot he'd kissed. "N-no problem," she stuttered. "Mom and I were catching up. She's just returned from Florida."

"Florida," he said, reaching up to touch his ear. "I used to own a condo in Miami."

His obviously unconscious gesture made her realize something was different between his right ear and his left. She didn't have time to dwell on the fact because she could tell by her mother's skeptical snort that Mom didn't believe him.

Escape, her brain cried. They needed to leave now

before Mom said something really humiliating. "Rufus, if you want, we could take off."

He smiled at her, warmly, then lifted her hand to his lips and kissed her knuckles. She was almost certain her knees weren't going to hold her, but then he turned to Mom and said, "Not yet. I haven't had a chance to talk to your mother. I spotted a quiet nook near the stairs…."

There was a hint of "I dare you" in his tone, and Rachel had never known her mother to walk away from a challenge.

Mom passed Rachel her highball glass—Jack Daniel's neat. "Very well."

As polite as any gentleman she'd ever met, Rufus escorted her mother out of sight. Rachel took a sip of the booze in her mother's glass, despite the fact she hated whiskey.

"What's going on?"

Coughing slightly, she glanced to her left to find her brother and future sister-in-law peering out of the kitchen. "I don't know. Mom and Rufus are talking. I'm pretty sure neither is armed, but you might want to put your finger on 9-1-1 speed dial just in case."

Jack laughed, but Kat seemed concerned. "I didn't even recognize Rufus at first. I had no idea he was so handsome. Jack's a little jealous, I think. Probably all the men are, but he doesn't seem to have eyes for anyone but you, Rachel."

"He's only living up to his side of our bargain."

Kat and Jack exchanged looks. "Pardon?" Kat asked.

"I hired him to be my date, Kat. Five hundred bucks. Well, two-fifty for tonight. The balance is to be my date at your wedding. So Mom can't carry on about what a loser I am."

Jack frowned. "You gave him money?"

"Not yet. We'll probably work out a trade." Jack's frown deepened. "Wait. That didn't come out right. What I meant is I'll credit the party against my hours updating his site."

"That sounds fair," Kat said, her tone anything but convincing.

Rachel shrugged. "He wore Armani. That has to be worth something, right? I know Mom was impressed even if she'd never in a million years admit it."

Jack put his arm around Kat. "I wish you didn't put so much stock in what Mom thinks. And she doesn't think you're a loser, Rae. She wants the best for you. For both of us. Sometimes she comes off a little opinionated."

Kat and Rachel looked at each other a moment, then both women rolled their eyes. "Jack, sweetheart," Kat said, hugging him fiercely. "Your selective blindness to the faults of the people you love is one of the things I adore most about you. But, seriously, Rosaline doesn't need a gun to draw blood, and not even Armani can stand up to a razor-sharp tongue."

Rachel stepped into the hallway, certain she'd be able to see her date and her mother near the staircase. "They're gone," she exclaimed. "Oh, no. I promised Rufus I'd protect him." She shoved Mom's glass at Jack. "If I'm not back in five minutes, call for help," she said dramatically.

CHAPTER ELEVEN

"YOU DON'T LIKE ME, do you, Mrs. Treadwell?"

The elegant woman sighed with affected ennui. "I don't have strong feelings one way or the other. I do, however, care deeply about my daughter. And I sincerely hope you are smart enough to see how emotionally fragile Rachel is. Her divorce was a bombshell. It wreaked havoc across every plane of her life. She's slowly picking up the pieces and doesn't need someone like you to come along and create more debris."

She delivered the speech as though she'd practiced it more than once—probably the entire length of the drive to the Black Hills from Denver. He refrained from applauding.

"I see. Then, you'll appreciate the fact that I'm her escort tonight not because she's madly and passionately attracted to me but because she paid me."

"I beg your pardon?"

"As you should. Rachel wanted to prove something to you, so she offered me money in return for my presence tonight and at your son's wedding. Ironic, isn't it?"

"What do you mean?"

He lowered his voice. "Rachel is one of the most capable and accomplished women I've ever met—and you're right in your unspoken assumption that I've known quite a few in my past life. But Rachel is unique. She's creative, authentic and vividly engaged in her work and the lives of the people she cares about. And, yet, when your name comes up, she represses that side of herself. Have you ever asked yourself why?"

"No, I haven't. Perhaps you'd like to enlighten me. You have no idea how much stock I put in a psychological profile divined by a reclusive, backwoods artisan in a borrowed Armani suit."

He threw back his head and laughed. "Sorry to disappoint you. It's my suit."

He could tell she didn't believe him. Her attitude baffled him. Unless she was acting this way out of fear.

The two young boys he'd been talking to earlier raced by, accidentally bumping against Rachel's mother. They tossed out their apologies but kept on running. Rufus took Rosaline's elbow and ushered her around the corner and out of the traffic flow. The back porch was conveniently empty. It wasn't as warm as the house, but he didn't intend to make this a long conversation.

"Mrs. Treadwell, I'm no psychologist, and I don't actually give a fig what you think about me. But your daughter is special. I haven't had a good friend in a long time. Rachel not only shook up my business, she made me reengage with people. That's her gift. Why can't you see that?"

"I beg to differ with you. She's a *gifted* accountant. Top of her class in college. She should be moving up the ladder in her chosen career, not wasting her time in Sentinel Pass." Her shiny red lips compressed in a moue of utter distaste. "It's bad enough I've lost my son to this joke of a town—a national joke, if you will. I won't stand idly by and watch my daughter throw away her future as well."

Anger—such a foreign emotion he almost didn't recognize it at first—blossomed in his belly. He clenched and unclenched his hands. First, she insulted her children, then his town. He took a step back to give himself breathing room. "Your job of child rearing is done. And, frankly, I think you did a great job. You have two wonderful, likeable children who are successes in their own right. And that's the point, isn't it? Once they're out of your house, it becomes about their lives and their successes."

"Are you a parent, Mr. Miller? No, of course not. You're a societal dropout. I hardly think that gives you any right to tell me how to be a parent to my children. Why am I even listening to you? You don't know my daughter."

"I know she saved me from losing something very important. She helped without ever asking what's in it for her. The answer is not very damn much. Hopefully enough money to make it worth her while and maybe— just maybe—make you proud of her. But honestly, I don't know why she bothers. You're never going to appreciate her."

She stepped forward as if preparing to slap his face. "How dare you say such a thing? You're not her boyfriend. You're nothing."

"If I were worthy of her, I'd be in line asking Rachel to consider me when she starts dating again. I'm not— worthy, that is—so you can relax. I'm sure a rustic artist with dubious income isn't up to your standard, but the point is you're not the one who counts here. Rachel is the only one who gets to pick." He met her eye-to-eye. "Are we clear on that?"

Rachel found her mother and Rufus in time to eavesdrop on their surprising conversation. She rarely heard Rufus utter more than half a dozen words in the same breath, let alone deliver a diatribe with such stone-cold authority it would have made a dead person sit up and pay attention.

Unfortunately, her mother was very much alive. And no one ever spoke to Rosaline Treadwell that bluntly—not bosses, coworkers, rebellious teens who might have wanted to shake things up and, especially, not Dad.

Rachel held her breath, one hand on the door, fully expecting fireworks. Instead, she heard a meek, resigned voice, say, "Yes, actually."

Rachel's jaw dropped. *Mom?*

"It's my fault about Trevor. Rachel's ex. I pushed them together even knowing his reputation. The golf world is pretty cloistered. I'd heard rumors that he was a playboy, but I thought Rachel would be able to whip him into shape, if you will. I made her doubt her instincts, which were dead on, and for that I will never forgive myself."

Wow. She looked around to find Jack, but he was across the room, sprawled on the floor with Kat's sons. She tried telepathy. *Jack. You have to hear this. Rufus did some kind of mind meld on Mom. She's definitely not herself. Hurry.* But he went on playing and laughing, impervious to her call.

"Hi, Rachel," a cheerful voice called—loud enough to out her to anyone standing beyond the doorway.

"Oh. Hi, Libby. Great party. I hope you don't mind

that I included Rufus without calling first. I meant to, but there's more to launching a new site than I realized."

Libby, hostess, book club diva and all-around great person, smiled benevolently. "I'm delighted that you brought Rufus. Who knew he was capable of pulling off such sartorial splendor? William told me Rufus reminded him of a model who used to appear in *GQ* magazine."

"Yep. Really something, huh?" *Then why do I like the old Rufus better?*

"Could I get your help a minute? Santa has arrived," she said with a wink, "and it seems we're experiencing a wardrobe malfunction. The last person to wear the suit must have been Rufus's height because the pant legs are about a foot too long." She paused in thought. "Or maybe the pants are one size fits all and they simply tuck the extra material into Santa's shiny black boots, but Eli wanted to wear moccasins, and he's going to trip and hurt himself if we don't make some modifications." She held up a roll of duct tape and grinned. "Gran's surefire fix-all."

Rachel hesitated. She needed to check on Rufus and make sure he was still in one piece. What if her mother had only been feigning humility before she went for the kill?

Libby patted her tummy. "I'd do it myself if I could bend over far enough."

"Sure. Lead the way. We can't let Santa wind up in the E.R. this close to Christmas."

Ten minutes later, after more laughter than she could possibly have expected—Eli was both handsome and charming—Rachel stood, shook out the towel she'd been kneeling on and looked around. "Okay," she said, smiling as she heard Eli's booming "Ho, ho, ho." coming from the living room. "Now, where's my date?"

Libby, who was leaning against the kitchen counter looking a little winded from running back and forth to keep her guests apprised of Santa's ETA, gave a small gasp.

"What?" Rachel asked, putting her hand on the other woman's forearm. "Labor pains?"

Libby shook her head. "No, no. Not that. It's Rufus. He left a few minutes ago. I thought you knew. He thanked me and said he had to get back to his work. I passed him heading this way. Maybe he saw how busy you were and…"

And he left without saying goodbye. "We have a lot of orders to fill," she said, trying not to sound as despondent as she felt.

Either that or Mom said something.

Libby nodded. "So I gathered. He gave you all the credit. Said you were a genius. I probably shouldn't say anything, but I think he might be sweet on you."

Rachel smiled at the old-fashioned term. "Sweet on me?"

Libby chuckled. "Sorry. I swear there are times I'm channeling Gran. You never got to meet her, did you?"

Rachel had heard a lot about the elder stateswoman of Sentinel Pass who passed away a few months earlier. "No. But everyone speaks very highly of her."

Libby's expressive face turned sad. "I miss her so much, but…we carry on. That's what we do. She was working part-time at the post office when Rufus first moved to town. She called him a lost soul in search of a place to put down roots. The Black Hills are home to lots of people like that."

"Like me," Rachel said softly, more to herself than Libby. She'd felt more at peace in the short time she'd been in the Hills than she ever had in Denver. Odd, she thought. Unless, it was less because of location and more a case of connection to one person.

"Libby, everyone calls you the wisest person around, can I ask you something?"

Libby laughed, her tone positively girlish. "Wise? Me? Who have you been talking to? Char? Don't believe her, she's in love. Love makes you silly."

Rachel didn't feel silly. She felt the exact opposite. Maybe that answered her question.

"But I'll happily give anyone advice on any topic— even something I know nothing about. Ask Cooper. He'll tell you."

"Tell her what?" her husband asked, slipping behind his wife to wrap his arms around her. "Good save on the Santa suit, Rachel," he added. "Eli even managed a Lakota dance of thanksgiving. Very cool."

"Happy to help."

"I told Rachel you'd agree that I'm rather opinionated."

Cooper's trademark blue eyes went wide. "Yes. I mean, no. I mean…is that a trick question?"

Rachel and Libby both laughed at his look of abject horror.

"Hey. It's not nice to tease people this close to Christmas. But, Rachel, I will say my wife is the most honest person you'll ever meet. So don't ask her a question unless you're prepared to hear the truth."

He gave his wife a tender hug and kiss on the cheek then winked at Rachel in a friendly, totally Cooper way before heading to the next room. He left the heavy swinging door open for Libby and Rachel to follow.

Libby waited, obviously sensing that Rachel had

more to talk about. She decided to leave her questions about Rufus until later. Once Cooper was out of earshot, she asked, "Do you think some people are walking black holes when it comes to relationships?"

Libby looked surprised by the question but she didn't hesitate to answer. "No. Absolutely not. Circumstance can trip us up, and we don't know what we need to learn until after we've been hit over the head with the lesson. That doesn't mean we're never going to get things right. Kat's a perfect example. She'd given up entirely on men, but look at her now. Have you ever seen anyone as happy as those two?"

Rachel turned and looked across the room. Kat had joined Jack on the floor and the two were laughing as they wrestled for control of the game. A lightness Rachel hadn't felt for a long time filled her with hope. Impulsively, she hugged Libby. "You're right. I'm a graduate of the school of hard knocks. Who among us isn't?"

Libby grinned. "Not Rufus. That's for sure. Gran called him a wounded bear. She predicted he'd come out of hibernation when the thorn in his paw was healed and not a day before." She winked. "Seeing him tonight, I'd say he's on the road to recovery. Wouldn't you?"

Rachel would, indeed. And she planned to track him down—after she had a word or two with her mother. "Thanks, Libby. I needed that pep talk. Now, one more question. Have you seen my mother?"

Libby glanced over shoulder. "I think she's out back. We borrowed one of those heaters from the teepee for the smokers in the group. I simply can't abide the smell."

Rachel's eyes opened wide. Her mother had given up

the habit when Dad was first diagnosed with cancer. As far as Rachel knew, Rosaline hadn't smoked since.

"Okay. Thanks. I'm going to take off, too, so I'd better let her know. It was a wonderful party. Thank you so much for inviting me."

She headed through the kitchen, a nervous hum in her chest, but stopped abruptly when the door opened and her mother stepped inside, a not unfamiliar aroma following her.

"Mom," Rachel exclaimed. "You're smoking?"

Mom waved away the accusation. "Of course not. I was talking to some gentleman, I can't remember is name. He was smoking. Not me."

She's lying. Rachel didn't know what to say.

"I might have bummed a drag or two," her mother confessed, still trying for blasé. "Were you looking for me for a reason? I thought you might have run off with your *date.*"

Deflection. The same tactic Trevor used when he was in trouble and wanted to keep the focus away from him.

A thought hit her. "Oh, my God. I married my mother."

Mom hung up her coat. "What are you talking about?"

"You know how they say girls always marry their fathers? Trevor is nothing like Dad. But he is an over-achiever in his chosen field, highly focused, a skilled ne-gotiator—he got me to marry him with an airtight prenup, didn't he?—and he's completely self-absorbed. Tell me if that doesn't sound more like you."

"I am not self-absorbed," Mom said, her pique obvious. "You and your brother have always been my main focus, except when I was trying to keep your father alive. Without much help from either of you, I might add."

That complaint again. "Mom, he was tired of fighting the cancer. The Big C was winning. I gave him permission to rest."

"To die, you mean. It wasn't yours to give, Rachel. He was my life, and unlike *your* husband, I was never unfaithful. So, you can keep your clever psychobabble to yourself. Which, I might add, is the same thing I told your client…excuse me, your hired date."

Back to Rufus. "I will gladly tell him that when I see him." She pretended to check her watch. "In twenty minutes or so. I'm going to make sure he got home safely."

Her mother snickered. "Is that a euphemism for booty call?"

Rachel tried not to look too shocked.

Rosaline picked up a glass that had her lip color on it around the rim. Her hand trembled slightly when she put it to her lips.

"Rufus is a great guy, Mom. He was kind enough to try to help me out tonight, and I really don't appreciate you pouncing on him like a mama lion taking down a young gazelle."

Her mother actually seemed pleased by the analogy but her smug smile fell when Rachel said, "So, I guess I have no choice but to drive to his place and offer what little succor I can to make up for your rudeness." She laid it on a little thick, but Rosaline got the message.

"I'll call him myself in the morning and apologize."

"A shame he doesn't have a phone."

"E-mail, then."

"You could try, but he's pretty busy filling Christmas orders. Tons of Christmas order. All from people thrilled to own a Rufus Miller original. Why…there's a chance he might be rich and famous some day, and aren't you going to kick yourself for not trying to play matchmaker to a guy who actually has some value?"

She could see she was wasting her breath. Her mother had one way of looking at things—Rosaline Treadwell's way. And, at the moment, Rachel didn't care what Rosaline Treadwell thought.

"Enjoy the rest of the party, Mom." Then she snatched her jacket from a coatrack, found her evening bag where she'd tucked it when she first arrived and exited through the same door her mother had used.

The frosty night made her breath resemble smoke, but when she looked toward the patio, she saw it was empty. No gentleman smoker.

She shook her head and let out a soft laugh. How ironic that her never-let-them-see-you-without-mascara mother was so discombobulated by a man who until a few hours earlier could have passed as Bigfoot's cousin that she broke any number of self-imposed rules by smoking in public.

Rachel knew her mother wasn't perfect, but it galled her that Mom could be so quick to judge others when her own flaws were simmering right below her faultless facade.

Rufus was the opposite. His appearance wasn't designed to impress anybody. But his hulking mountain-man look was every bit as contrived as her mother's. Who was the real Rufus Miller? Was that even his real name? She doubted it, despite the fact that she'd seen his driver's license.

She was sick and tired of men who pretended to be one thing but turned out to be something completely different. And she damn well planned to tell him so.

CHAPTER TWELVE

RUFUS PACED HIS LIVING ROOM, debating about taking a bath. Maybe the hot water would help calm the turbulent, edgy feelings that hummed through his veins.

"Too much rich food," he told his dogs, who watched him with perplexed looks.

Or too many toasts of champagne. Good champagne, too. He hadn't expected to be able to tell the difference, but he still could.

He'd liked that rush of crisp, dry bubbles that almost burned as it cascaded over his tongue. If he was honest, the alcohol—something he'd denied himself since his diagnosis—wasn't the only thing he'd enjoyed.

He stopped and turned to look at his reflection in the window. He'd removed his jacket and rolled up the sleeves of his silk shirt when he got home. His feet were complaining from being squeezed into shoes that looked stylish but weren't made for comfort. He hadn't kicked them off the moment he walked in the door. Why, he wondered?

He shifted slightly. A subtle, ultra-casual pose. One of his signature looks.

Did he miss modeling?

He shook his head, conscious of how different it felt to have his hair tamed with gel and styled in a way that was all too familiar. He was positive he no longer felt any pull toward that part of his former life.

He reached up and yanked the rubber band from his hair. He pushed it into his hip pocket then bent over to shake his hair loose. It felt stiff with product, but he figured if his scalp could breathe again the dull pulsing pain in his head might go away.

Straightening, he closed his eyes from a momentary rush of blood. When he looked at his reflection again, he saw a more familiar face. No beard, but it would grow back. And, in all honesty, he didn't miss it.

He couldn't deny that he had derived a certain thrill from feeling handsome again. As ridiculous and shallow as that sounded, he'd enjoyed watching people's expressions when they saw him for the first time. Surprise, interest, praise, desire.

The last had been obvious in Rachel's eyes. And the feeling had been mutual.

Her sexy red dress had reminded him of a candle flame—mesmerizing and hot. Had he liked the lust and admiration he'd read in her eyes? Hell, yes. His first impulse had been to sweep her into his arms and carry her, caveman-style, to a remote corner and make out until dawn.

But those raw, unguarded emotions were exactly what he'd been attempting to avoid all these years. Bad things happened when you took your eye off the ball. And all the money, fame, beautiful women and booze in the world couldn't fix you. His New York lifestyle had been as big a sham as this one was, only it cost more.

Literally and emotionally. He'd paid the price in terms of health and self-respect.

Talking to Rachel's mother had made him realize how important Rachel had become to him. How much she'd changed things in such a short time. And understanding that, he'd reacted much the same way he had after his agent pulled the rug out from under him. He'd run.

So much for the Zen of personal growth.

He turned his back on his reflection. One of his mother's favorite sayings had been, "The more things change, the more they stay the same." He understood that, now.

Rachel's mother was right—if for the wrong reasons. He needed to put a halt to the attraction between him and Rachel. For both their sakes. He knew from experience that rebound affairs rarely lasted. Only a pathetic fool would start something that was bound to end badly.

"I need to focus on business," he told his dogs.

All three sets of ears perked up, impressed, no doubt, by his decisive tone.

He kicked off his shoes and charged up the spiral staircase. He had a new plan. He'd build Dreamhouses all night and sleep during the day when Rachel was in her office. He wouldn't back out of their agreement, even if it killed him to be around her.

An hour later, he pushed his current project away with a snarl of frustration. "Damn."

His focus was a mess. He was tempted to blame the alcohol but he knew better. It was Rachel. The memory of her smile the moment she realized the stranger in the nice suit was Rufus was one he couldn't quit replaying in his head. Her shapely legs and sexy heels. The way her dress clung to her womanly shape. The wounded-kitten look in her eyes when her mother harangued her.

With a grunt of capitulation, he stood.

He checked the clock. Eleven-thirty. Too early to go to bed, too late to start a bath.

After tossing a couple of logs in the wood-burning stove, he trudged back to his workbench. The dogs hadn't moved from their cozy spots by the fire. He didn't blame them. Today had been a long, confusing day. He halfway wished he had a few pharmaceuticals in his medicine cabinet. Doctors were always happy to prescribe drugs for celebrities.

He stopped at the foot of the steps that led to the second floor. "Maybe I'd feel more inspired if I saw some of the new orders," he murmured.

Pausing at the landing, he looked around. The place had Rachel's stamp on it everywhere, neat and orderly yet fun. Two bumper stickers were tacked to the bulletin board a foot or so to the right of her desk. One read Namaste. The other said The Drink in Front of Me is Cheaper Than a Frontal Lobotomy."

He snickered at that.

He bypassed the U-shaped packing center and walked straight to her desk. Her laptop was open. He settled into her chair and moved the mouse to activate the computer. He smiled at her wallpaper—one of his Dreamhouses. His fingers hovered over the icon that would take him directly to his new Web site.

After a few seconds of silent debate, he clicked on a popular search engine icon, instead. At the prompt, he typed in his former professional name: R. J. Milne.

To his surprise, the search revealed several hundred links, ranging from official fan club to dozens of magazine attributions. One in particular caught his eye: *R. J. Milne voted sexiest kisser in print ad.*

He clicked on it. A second later the screen was filled with an image of his body, clad only in the briefest of white briefs, kneeling over a voluptuous woman in a string bikini. Their lips were barely touching but the connection seemed to cry hot sex.

If he closed his eyes, he could picture the shoot. Mid-November. Colder than hell. A drafty midtown Manhattan warehouse. The photographer was famous—and infamous. He traveled with no less than fourteen flunkies and he shrieked at them constantly, using profanities unlike anything Rufus had heard up to that time. The female model had the best body money could buy, but Rufus had seen her pop a handful of pills—he didn't know or care what kind—dry, no water, right before they started posing. Even a few ounces of water might show up as bloat if you weren't careful, he'd once heard a female model say.

"Did you screw her?" a voice asked from behind him.

His momentary jolt of shock dissipated quickly once he glanced over his shoulder. Rachel. He'd been so engrossed in his trip down memory lane he hadn't heard her come in. And, neither, apparently, had his ferocious guard dogs.

"Not so much as a whimper," he muttered under his breath as he turned to look at her.

She must have come straight from the party because she was still wearing her slinky red dress under her puffy jacket. It was a cold night and nylons couldn't have provided much warmth. He started to stand, intending to lead the way to the fire, but she stopped him. "That is you, isn't it? I don't recognize the name, but the rest of you looks familiar."

He glanced at the screen. "I didn't sleep with her," he said, truthfully. "Not for lack of trying, but my agent failed to tell me this was a one-on-one shot. Afterward, I heard that she referred to me as 'scampi breath'."

The corners of her mouth flickered but she didn't smile. "You left the party without saying goodbye. That's really bad date etiquette—especially when there's money on the line."

"I know. I planned to apologize in the morning."

"That's not good enough. I couldn't spend the rest of the night wondering what I did to make you leave."

A knifelike pain caught him right under the sternum. Good Lord, it never occurred to him she'd blame herself, but it made sense. Wasn't she still beating herself up about her divorce? Even though her lowlife ex deserved the majority of the blame?

"It wasn't your fault, Rachel."

She crossed her arms. "So what happened? Did Mother verbally rip you to shreds? Was the crowd too much? What?" She put out one hand before he could answer. "If you tell me you found another woman, I'll be right back with a gun."

He had to grip the arms of the chair to keep from launching himself across the space between them to take her in his arms. "It was me, Rachel. Just me. I think I had a mild panic attack."

Instantly, her expression turned sympathetic, and she took a step forward. Now, it was his turn to hold up a hand. "I thought I could handle a small social gathering like that, but apparently not. When your mother and I finished our discussion, she went outside and I went looking for you. Someone said you were in the kitchen with Santa." He paused, wondering if he should mention the spurt of jealousy that ripped through him. An emotion so foreign and unexpected, he felt a momentary burst of panic.

"I was fixing Eli's borrowed costume."

He nodded. "I know. I saw you." Laughing and joking with an insider's ease. Something he'd never known and always envied. Even at the height of his popularity and earning power, he'd felt like a fake. A fraud. A small-town rube who would be kicked back to South Dakota when the truth came out. "Men in red suits scare me," he joked.

He could tell she didn't believe him.

"Have you seen a doctor for the problem? They make drugs for—" She stepped closer. "Why are you smiling?"

"Doctors and I don't get along. I've seen more than my share. I'm healthy, productive, self-sufficient…as long as I stay within my comfort zone and avoid all things Christmas. What's wrong with that?"

She stuck her hands in her pockets and frowned. "Nothing, I guess. If that's all you want out of life. But I watched you tonight, Rufus. You worked the room like a social networking pro. Everyone was blown away—partly by your looks, partly by how friendly and easygoing you were. Most said they'd never seen that side of you. Were you acting?"

The question gave him pause. He wasn't sure how to answer. "I used to be the king of schmooze. I could talk to anybody. People—especially women—were always hanging around me. Now, it's me and the dogs. They don't require a lot of small talk."

"You don't seem uncomfortable talking to me. Is that an act, too? Has my presence been a burden and you were too polite to say so?"

He could tell that idea hurt her. "No. You're different than most people. You and Kat both accept me the way I am."

She rolled her eyes. "Right," she said dryly. "You mean until the moment I asked you to shave your beard and pretend to be someone you're not."

But who am I? Is it possible there's still some of the old R. J. Milne in me?

"I was certain that was why you left without saying goodbye. Because you were mad at me. Hiring you to be my date was dumb, but asking you to shave and be someone you're not was worse. I really am sorry, Rufus."

He believed her, but before he could tell her that he didn't regret being her date, she added, "But you do look great. Not that you looked bad with a beard, but… well…the other Rufus definitely wouldn't have been posing with that woman—bad breath or not."

To keep her from seeing his smile, he spun the chair around and tapped the mouse on the little *X* in the upper corner of the page. He quickly backed out of his search and opened the Dreamhouses Web site.

"I was going to check on new orders. I thought having a deadline might inspire me."

Her heels made a crisp, all-business staccato on the floor as she cleared the distance between them. In his peripheral vision, he could see the shimmer of her elegant hosiery. "Go to the drop-down menu at the top and click Orders."

He did. As they waited for the information to appear, she hopped up on the desk. "I saw the lights on in the house, but I didn't stop. I knew you'd be here," she told him, slipping off her jacket.

Her cocktail-length dress had long, fitted sleeves. It might have been warm, if not for the plunging neckline in back.

"Why?"

"Partly because you told Libby you had orders to fill and partly because work is my escape, too."

He had to ask. "Did you and your mother have words?"

She threw up her hands with a look of consternation. "What is with all this old-fashioned, euphemistic talk?"

He had no idea what she meant so he didn't say anything.

"Mom and I have two ways of communicating. Twitteresque—short and businesslike," she explained. "Or in-your-face contentious. No middle ground. I don't know why that is. Even when I'm trying to be a model daughter, she's not happy with me. She doesn't say so out loud, but when Mom is talking to me, I hear words like *foolish, bullheaded, infantile, self-centered* and *inconsiderate* in the subtext."

"You aren't any of those things as far as I can see. Have you tried telling her that?"

She shrugged, which made the fabric covering her left shoulder edge downward exposing more of her smooth, creamy neck. "It would probably help if we spoke the same language, but we don't. She's smart and pragmatic and practical. I'm more of a fly-by-the-seat-of-your-pants girl. Mom hates not having a plan. I've never met a plan that didn't need tweaking."

He smiled at her answer. Maybe that was the reason he liked her so much. Because he knew all too well that the best laid plans weren't worth the price of the paper they were written on. Stephen would attest to that. If he were still alive.

She leaned down to see the screen, so he angled the unit more her way. With a couple of key strokes, she brought up the newest orders. Several included comments in the box she'd thoughtfully provided for customer feedback.

He read the first one.

I luv these things. Smart idea. You saved my butt where buying a gift for my sister is concerned. Merry Xmas.
Dave.

"We've gotten a lot like that," she said. "But there's one in here that you'll really like."

She scooted sideways for balance. Her left leg hung down but her right curled under her slightly, opening a gap above her knees. Rufus gulped and intensified his focus on the screen.

She leaned closer, her perfume beckoning.

"Here it is."

She turned the screen his way. Rufus had to blink twice to remember what he was supposed to be doing. Reading. Regaining his purpose and focus. *Right.*

The note was brief.

My mom is sick. I'm gonna write a get-well note every night to put in this Dreamhouse. Some hope is better than none. Thank you and God bless.

"Sweet, huh?"

"Sad," he said, closing the screen.

She nodded. "Can you tell me why you went from the man in that photo to hiding behind long hair and a beard?"

He rocked back in the chair and sighed. "When I first started modeling, I did a lot of underwear ads. But what they were really selling was sex." He snorted. "You weren't far off when you called me a gigolo."

"Why'd you quit?"

"Overexposure." True, because overexposure to tanning beds and beach shoots probably contributed to his cancer. But he wasn't ready to talk about that. He'd swallowed a lifetime of sympathy after Stephen died. He didn't need or want hers.

She didn't say anything for a minute. "So, you shucked your modeling career to move to the Black Hills. You must have been pretty successful if you could afford to build a new home and a shop and not work for several years."

"I made a lot of money."

"Wouldn't you call that successful?"

He rubbed his jaw with his thumb, lost for a second in how soft and strange his skin felt. Her cough brought him back to her question. "When you're young and caught up in a glamorous lifestyle, it takes a while to figure out that wealth doesn't equal happiness—no matter what people want to believe."

Her expression turned sad. "You won't get an

argument from me on that one. But now you're working hard again to earn money. What happened to your funds? Taxes? Bad investments?"

"The latter."

"Bummer."

He smiled at the understanding look in her eyes. She was a caring, generous person. Honest, too. Too bad he hadn't hired her to handle his money back in the day. He might have, if he'd known her at the time.

A small regret in a lifetime of big ones.

"So, your former career choice is your deep, dark secret?"

One of them. "Why tell people about your past when it's over? I burned my bridges when I came here. Libby's grandmother told me the Hills are tolerant of people who come here to start again. Isn't that why you came?"

She sat up primly. Sexy and proper at the same time. Not a look that was easy to pull off, but she did so with aplomb.

"I definitely needed a fresh start. Sentinel Pass was the most likely choice because I'm too big a coward to strike out on my own." He heard her mother behind that comment and didn't like it. "In my own defense, however, having my brother nearby makes sense from a client-building and contact-list point of view, wouldn't you agree?"

He nodded, not trusting himself to speak. She might have issues with her mother, but he knew from experience that no matter how difficult and convoluted someone's relationship with a parent, they'd defend them to the death.

"But I didn't come here to talk about myself."

"Why did you come?"

Her lips pursed. "To make sure you were okay. My ex called Mom a vampire cheerleader because every pep talk ends with bloodletting."

He snickered at that. "Your mother reminded me of my former agent, Marianne. I overheard someone call her cold to her face and she replied that everything she knew about business she learned from a man."

"Hmm. Interesting. Dad always said Mom was the strong one in the family." Her thumb fiddled absently with her bottom lip. Reminding him of how much he'd enjoyed kissing her. "Jack and I weren't allowed to criticize her around Dad. Even when she was pushing him to fight a battle he couldn't win." She shook her head. "A long, sad story. I should go."

"You can't," he said. "Didn't you tell me you needed at least an hour after driving down my road to stop your teeth from rattling?"

She smiled. "I did say that, didn't I? I guess I'm getting used to it. I've made so many trips lately, and it gets dark so early these days, I think I could drive it in my sleep."

He waited to see if she'd hop down and grab her coat, but she didn't. She simply sat there looking lost and a bit befuddled. She needed a hug, and he was going to give her one—even if physical contact was in direct violation of his earlier, set-in-stone mandate.

He stood and closed the distance between them in a single step. He might have been able to resist her body—he'd seen some of the most beautiful women in the world up close and minimally clothed—but he was powerless against her vulnerability.

"Oh," she said, surprised but not alarmed. She

hugged him back in a friendly, not particularly provocative way. "Nice. I like your cologne."

"Thank you."

"But I think I like your wood-and-glue smell better." Her eyes went wide and she pulled away. "Uh-oh. Does that make me a huffer?"

He grinned and shook his head. "I don't think so. Secondhand glue fumes are not addictive."

Their gazes met and held. Rufus knew that in addition to vulnerability, he was also a complete and utter sucker for a beautiful mind. Not only smart, but quick, nimble, supple and open. Her thought process reminded him of the way he built birdhouses. Testing, twisting, reshaping bits and pieces of nature until he had something interesting and unique.

In the past few months, his motto had become "try everything because you never know what will fit best."

Try everything… He put his hand on her knee. The fabric of the hem was luxurious, but not was silky as her sheer stockings. She drew in a small, quick gulp of air.

"I thought touching was bad form. Unprofessional."

He shrugged. "For you, maybe. But I think there's a law that says clients don't have to be professional. Want me to show you just how unprofessional I can get?"

She swallowed loudly. The tip of her tongue moistened her lips as she weighed the offer.

He didn't wait for an answer. He leaned in to kiss her. She didn't kiss him back, but she didn't push him away, either.

Through half-closed lids, he watched her react to his persistent little nibbles on her full bottom lip. His nose nuzzled her cheek as his hand squeezed her knee, slipping ever so casually under the hem, inching upward until he touched skin.

He froze. "Speaking of anachronisms? Are you wearing a garter belt and hose?"

Her expression turned impish. "You saw my box of sex toys. I figured you knew I was a scandalous hussy. Black lace and stockings are only the beginning. Are you sure you want to go there?"

He knew damn well that he shouldn't. There would be hell to pay in the morning...or somewhere down the road. But he couldn't stop now. "Black lace? My complete and utter downfall. Can I peek?"

She threw her arms around him and opened her legs to draw him close. "Oh, hell, I give up. You can do a lot more than that."

He lowered his head and sealed the deal to the best offer he'd ever had.

Rachel knew she was going to regret this impulsive act. It wasn't as bad as marrying a man she barely knew, but having sex with a client had to be up there.

It wasn't too late to stop, she told herself. Rufus might be many things, including a sexy stud in lumberjack clothing, but he wasn't the kind of man who needed to win at all cost. He would have listened to her protests and stepped away...if she wanted to protest.

But she didn't. His work-roughened hands added the perfect amount of friction against her skin. His touch was sure and firm, as if following a creative muse to a wonderful piece of work.

"Should we go to the house?" he asked, dropping a shower of kisses down the side of her neck as he eased the fabric from across one shoulder.

She shivered, but not from the cold. She'd always had a secret fantasy about making love on a desk. "No. I want to stay here."

His left eyebrow lifted in surprise. "Here here?"

She moved her hips to scoot forward until their bodies touched. Right where they needed to touch. "Uh-huh."

He didn't say anything but a slow, all-knowing smile pulled up one corner of his mouth. His really beautiful mouth. She put her thumb to his lips and ran it along the edge of his teeth. He sucked it in playfully, grinning as he did.

"I have the feeling you're going to be full of surprises."

"Nope. What you see is exactly what you get. Nothing more. Not a whole lot less," she said, glancing down at her chest, which probably looked a bit perkier than normal because of her the dress's clever underwire support.

"That works for me," he said. He lifted her hand and kissed the back of it while looking into her eyes. "Because what I see is pretty damn fantastic."

She was about to say, "I bet you say that to all your Web designers," but decided against it. She didn't want either of them to be reminded of work. This wasn't about the mundane world. This was about fantasy and escape.

"I should warn you…it's been a while for me."

In the muted light, his eyes were the color of dark chocolate. Her favorite. "Me, too. But I'm pretty sure the mechanics will come back to us," he said.

The low, sexy edge to his voice sent a rush of desire through her blood. At this point, she'd take good, bad or otherwise. She wanted him. Period. But she wasn't a fool. "Do we need to have the safe-sex talk?" she asked.

He looked at her soberly. "A few years ago, I would have said, 'Absolutely,' where I was concerned. But one good thing about leading a monkish life is you have no communicable diseases to communicate. You?"

She made a pretend Girl Scout pledge. "Clean bill of health, top to bottom. The one good thing about having a cheating husband is you don't take anything for granted, health-wise. And pregnancy isn't an issue because I'm in year two of a three-year birth control implant." *Thank you, Trevor.*

If she was afraid such frank, unromantic talk might cast a damper on his ardor, she was wrong. His expression turned roguish and heartthrob sexy. Suddenly she understood why he'd been such a successful model—the man was hot.

And he wanted her. She sensed that at every level. The anticipation nearly robbed her of speech. "So, we're good?"

He edged the shoulder of her dress an inch or so lower using his index finger. "Oh, yeah. We're good... and we're going to get bad. Very bad," he said with a throaty growl that made her blood pulse.

And, although she was mildly surprised, she also knew she was ready. Fun, frivolous and fantastic sex. She'd take any—or all—of the above. Without regret, she promised herself. No second-guessing and whining. She deserved this.

CHAPTER THIRTEEN

FINESSE. THAT HAD always been his policy. Even when he was three sheets to the wind after a long night of partying and there was a good chance he wouldn't remember the name of the woman in his arms the next morning, he made damn sure she'd remember him. He'd take his time, petting, kissing, licking—whatever and wherever—until she was putty in his hands.

But the instant Rachel gave him the okay to make love with her, he knew things were going to be different. Because it had been so long for him? He didn't think so. More it was about what she did to him. Her touch sent crazy shivers throughout his body. When she started to unbutton his shirt he went as hard as a teenager with his first nudie magazine.

And she felt it. How could she not since he was pressed against the *V* of her legs. They were both still completely dressed but she had a lot less to remove than he did. She shimmied closer.

"You excite me."

"I can tell."

He pulled back enough to put his hand where his body had been. He cupped her, pressing the heel of his hand against the heated, dewy resistance of her panties.

Rolling his palm in a slow, firm circle, he drew a slight gasp that turned to a purr.

She let go of his shoulders and leaned back on her elbows. Neck arched, she moved her hips harder and faster, her body telling him what she wanted and needed. After a few seconds, he slipped his middle finger under the elastic of her bikinis and found her, hot and ready.

"Oh," she cried, her eyes flying open.

She held her breath and rode the sensation as he explored, tested and teased.

The silky material of the dress fell back, bunching around the tops of her thighs. He pushed it higher, exposing the pretty white flesh of her belly. There was a faint bikini line defined by her skimpy lace panties but he was glad to see she didn't go in for the year-round-tan look.

He leaned over and kissed her belly button, his hands silently praising her womanly shape. He'd made love to enough rail-thin models to prefer a softer, more natural body. Rachel's was perfect. And he told her so.

He could tell by the look in her eyes she didn't believe him. He would have to prove it by worshipping every aspect of her…if he could hold out that long.

She stroked the side of his cheek with the tips of her fingers a moment. Then she sat up and reached behind her back. He heard the distinctive sound of a zipper. A second later, the bodice of her dress gaped provocatively.

The dress had a built-in bra, he realized, catching glimpses of her beautiful, upturned breasts, as she slipped her arms free of the long sleeves. The reciprocal surge in desire nearly unmanned him. He sucked in his gut and tried to think of something else.

Dogs. Where were his dogs?

"Ooh," she said, clasping the fabric to her chest. "Cooler than I thought." She smiled. "Probably because I'm so overheated from the inside out."

He quickly finished unbuttoning his shirt and wrenched it off to drape across her shoulders. Plaid flannel and red silk—an odd combination. But somehow it worked. She smiled as if he'd given her diamonds.

"You are incredible," he said, mesmerized by her loveliness.

Grinning, she kicked off her shoes. They clattered on the floor, causing one of the dogs to let out a half-hearted woof.

She wrapped her legs around him and reached up to rest her forearms on his shoulders. His shirt was forgotten, and Rufus knew they weren't going to need the warmth it might provide. The heat between them could have fueled the workshop all night.

"Are you sure you don't want a soft bed?" he asked, praying she would say no. "Or the sofa by the fire?"

"Later," she answered. Her voice low and throaty. She licked her lips and said, "I need you to make love to me. Now."

That he could handle.

He kissed her, pressing his tongue deep into her mouth then flicking and teasing. She liked to play, too. He could tell by the way she raked her fingers through his hair and nipped at his bottom lip.

When they were both thoroughly aroused, he unbuttoned his jeans and carefully lowered the zipper. He'd been in a hurry when he changed clothes and hadn't bothered with underwear. Or so he'd told himself.

Maybe he'd been hoping against hope that something like this might happen.

Whatever *this* was. Consensual sex between two people who didn't have anything to lose?

Except, well…everything.

But he was way past the point of no return, and he was pretty sure whatever emotional price making love with Rachel Grey took from him would be worth it.

He attempted to release the garters, but his fingers felt out of touch with his brain. Rachel guided his hands as if he might not be familiar with such things. He doubted there was a single article of women's clothing he hadn't removed at one time or another, but her naiveté made him stop. He could fall hard for this woman, he realized.

"Something wrong?" she asked. "Is the hook in back stuck? Just rip it."

Her tone was faintly peeved. She wanted him as much as he wanted her. Want wasn't the same as love. He knew that fact all too well.

Want was safe.

He wrenched the last, uncooperative hook free then tossed the sexy scrap of material over his shoulder, not giving a damn where it landed. "How valuable are these stockings?"

She looked confused. "Valuable? Oh. You mean do I want to wear them again?"

He held up his wood-roughened hands. "They'd probably fare better with sandpaper."

She took the right one in her hands, cradling it lovingly. She kissed his calluses. "The nylons are ridiculously expensive. I bought them when I was married. You can cut them off if you prefer."

He believed her. And that little hint that she was over her ex was oddly liberating. He started with the right leg and slowly inched the silky material downward, kissing the inside of her thigh, knee and calf as he went.

Her breathing sped up and her nipples puckered. "Nice," she whispered.

He repeated the process on the left leg. This time keeping the stocking. He dangled the toe above her belly, dragging it ever so softly across the nest of dark red curls. She arched her back and moved her hips, provocatively.

The pheromones that nature provided were released on a bouquet of pure desire. He dropped the stocking and put his hands on either side of her hips. Were there elements of foreplay he was skipping? Hell, yes. Was he rushing ahead of himself in a way the old Rufus never would have rushed? Right, again. But the fact was he'd never felt this clutch of desire before. He couldn't wait to feel her body wrapped around him.

His highly vaulted self-control was shot.

Not that she seemed to mind.

Rachel gasped when he finally entered her. Not from pain or surprise but from sheer relief. One part of her mind took stock of the image they made—papers scattered, desk topsy-turvy while two healthy, mostly naked people made love with abandon. Yes, she silently cheered. Another fantasy fulfilled.

Here she was. Intensely alive. Making love with one of the sexiest men she'd ever met. And he was completely focused on pleasuring her.

If she wasn't so intent on what was happening inside her body, she might have wept with gratitude.

Thank you, thank you, thank you. Not for pleasuring

her, although he did—immensely—but because she could tell he needed this, too. And she was pretty sure he needed *her.* That was the best validation of all.

"You…feel…perfect," she panted, concentrating on the rhythm taking hold inside her.

He reached under her, grasping her hips with his big, strong hands. His eyes were closed, his face intensely focused. His chest was heaving as he matched her steadily growing crescendo.

She'd had orgasms before. She knew what to expect. She turned herself over to the feeling and waited for the pleasant crest to come and go.

But that wasn't how it happened. The pulsing burst of color that shattered behind her closed eyes was only the beginning. Wave after wave of mind-blowing pleasure rocketed through her body, reaching every fiber of her being. Her breath stopped. She might even have blacked out for a millisecond. But, oh, what a way to go.

Her triumph carried a special, unspoken relief because there'd been a time during the divorce when she'd felt as ugly, unsexy and valueless as Trevor had wanted her to feel.

Breathing hard, struggling for cognitive powers of speech, she finally managed to say, "Holy cow."

His low rumble passed through her, too, as he rested against her. He hadn't collapsed on top of her. No. He was too mindful of squishing her. She knew that and the knowledge made her feel sheltered, protected and loved.

She swallowed loudly.

Rufus lifted his head. "Am I hurting you?"

"No. I'm good. Really, really good, actually. That was fantastic. You have no idea."

"I think I do. I was there, too, remember?"

She snickered softly. "I know, but it's different for a guy. Isn't it?"

He made a face. "I don't know. I've never been a woman. But I can tell you that was…unmatched in my experience." He looked slightly chagrined when he added, "And, believe me, that says a lot."

SHE MIGHT HAVE ASKED him to explain, but he didn't give her a chance. He stepped backward. Used his shirt to tidy her up, first, then himself. "I left another one hanging on the work bench," he said. "I'll go grab it and put a couple more logs on the fire. Can I get you anything?"

She levered herself up on her elbows and watched him pull on his jeans and slip his bare feet into his work boots, sans socks. The chilly air finally made itself known. Her nipples puckered when she looked down at her naked body.

The fire was definitely in need of another log. "Could you fill the electric kettle with water?" she asked, pointing toward the three-drawer file cabinet where she'd set up a hot water dispenser. "A cup of cocoa sounds heavenly."

"Sure. No problem."

Once she was alone, she hopped off the desk and pulled on her panties. As she reached for her dress, a shiver passed through her. It wasn't just chilly, it was cold. A cocktail dress didn't sound all that appealing at the moment.

"Wait a minute," she murmured, turning toward the stack of boxes she'd brought with her the other day. None was particularly well-marked—thanks to Jack—but, if she wasn't mistaken, one contained her gym bag.

She found it immediately. Sure enough, right on top was her turquoise-and-white Nike bag. *With any luck…*

"Halleluiah." Black jogging pants, a Coors Light T-shirt, a hoodie, socks and—best of all—tennis shoes.

She and Trevor had planned to start playing tennis twice a week. He'd made their first date but forgot the second. There wasn't a third because that weekend she'd caught him with another woman.

As she zipped the jacket, she took stock of how she felt about what happened to her marriage. She'd been devastated, at first. She'd grieved. And now…she was done thinking about any of it.

She started to smile. She was healed, and the man trotting up the stairs at that moment had a lot to do with her transformation. She planned to tell him that.

Well, maybe not everything she felt. Goodness, the poor guy would probably run for the woods and never return. But she could thank him. At least one more time.

CHAPTER FOURTEEN

"I SHOULD GO," SHE said a few hours later.

"Why? Aren't you planning to work tomorrow? I mean today?" he asked, drawing her a little bit tighter into the warm, safe cocoon of his arms. With her head resting on his bare chest, she felt a languid comfort pulling her toward sleep.

But her conscience—or was that her mother's voice in her head?—nagged her to get up, get dressed and go home. Having consensual sex with a client was one thing, sleeping over was another.

"Today is Sunday."

"You're going to church to repent your sins." His tone held an element of teasing, but something else, too.

"No. My family isn't particularly religious. Are you?"

"Used to be. Grew up Lutheran. Now, I'm not."

Her sleepiness receded. "Because of what happened to your brother?"

He didn't answer right away. "I suppose so. Everything changed when he died. I can barely even remember what our lives were like before the accident. What I was like."

She rose to look him in the eyes. "You didn't mention how he died. Car?"

"No. That probably would have been easier to accept. It was a fluke. He was horsing around with friends and fell off the bleachers in the gym. Not even that high. Maybe four feet, at most. He didn't pass out or anything. He bounced to his feet, laughing. But later that night, he threw up and said his head ached." He swallowed. "The doctors did surgery to repair a broken blood vessel in his brain, but he never regained consciousness."

"Oh, my gosh. How horrible."

"He was in a coma for four months. Mom went to the hospital every day. Some nights she stayed in the homes of church folk who took her in, but most of the time she made the drive by herself because my dad... He didn't handle it well." He heaved a sigh. "Stephen was the glue that kept us together. Without him, we fell apart."

She understood all too well. Did tragedy magnify the dysfunctional tendencies in a family?

"My dad blamed me for Stephen's fall."

A stab of pain arced through her. "Why?"

"I'd finished practice and was hanging around with some friends. Girls. Stephen was at that age where he wanted a share of the attention, too. He was showing off for a girl in his class. She had a crush on me."

"That's not your fault."

"I know, but when a young person dies, there's never a shortage of guilt to go around."

She pressed her body against his and hugged him fiercely. "I'm sorry that happened to you. To your family."

He nuzzled the top of her head with his chin. His voice was low and sexy when he said, "Me, too. Does this mean you're staying?"

"Oh, heck, I've broken so many rules, what's one more? Yes, I'll stay."

He kissed her forehead. "Good. I'll make you breakfast in the morning.

"Pine needles and berries?"

He grinned. "You'll see. Now, we'd better grab a couple of hours of sleep so we're not completely worthless tomorrow. Your most excellent Web site is attracting a lot of new orders."

His praise was nice to hear, but her brain was already shutting down. Her last conscious thought was *I could get used to this.*

BREAKFAST THE NEXT MORNING was a happy surprise. No bark, pine needles or dried berries in sight.

"Pancakes? From scratch? I'm impressed."

"Sourdough. A friend gave me the starter as a housewarming gift. I make them at least once a week. The dogs love them."

The idea astounded her. Probably because none of the men in her life had ever shown the least bit of culinary interest or aptitude.

The dogs seemed happily at ease in the kitchen with their master. Another first for her. Mom wasn't an animal lover and claimed to have allergies. Pets had been verboten in the Treadwell home.

"The coffee is excellent. Thank you," she said, noticing he'd added a small thermal coffee press to the minimalist clutter on his counter.

"You're welcome."

The smell of pancakes made her mouth water. She stirred some cream into the mug then said, "Can I ask you something? It's personal. And not really any of my business."

He looked over his shoulder. He'd pulled his trimmed hair into a ponytail at the back of his neck. "I'd say you're entitled to at least two personal questions." A reference, she assumed, to the number of times they'd made love the night before.

"The envelope that Cooper held up last night at the gifting tree looked familiar. Was that your thousand-dollar donation?"

His shoulders tensed. He didn't look at her when he said, "Yes. I've never made any effort to spread the word about Stephen's House locally. I did a lot of PR in the beginning, when I figured my celebrity would do some good. Once I moved to the Hills, I kept my involvement limited to writing checks. But, as I think I told you, the seed money for the furnishings wound up being part of a Ponzi scheme."

She hopped off her stool and walked to him. She wrapped her arms around his middle and squeezed. "My ex lost a bundle to that guy. Or so he claimed in our divorce papers. Things like that are always going to happen, Rufus. You don't have any control over other people's greed."

He relaxed a little, but kept his attention trained on the griddle. "Cooper promised to make a list of the charities from last night to circulate amongst his well-heeled friends. The more money I can help to raise, the less I have to worry about making through my art."

"That's nothing to worry about. Your Dreamhouses are going to sell out. I'm absolutely certain."

He didn't say anything but he was smiling when he

turned to face her. "Pancakes are ready. I hope you're hungry. I tripled the recipe."

She jumped back. "Tripled? Do I look starved?"

"The dogs would be crushed if they didn't get their share. Sourdough is highly digestible and good for dogs, too."

Each of the three beasts had their mouths open with tongues hanging out in obvious expectation. She couldn't help but laugh. Unexpected joy bubbled up through her being. What a wonderful gift Rufus had turned out to be—and it wasn't even Christmas.

Rufus was midway through his second helping when Rachel voiced her second question—the one he'd been expecting earlier.

"Why'd you really quit modeling?"

After the connection they'd shared the night before he had no choice but to answer honestly. "I was diagnosed with skin cancer. My doctor found a malignant melanoma on my ear." He turned his head to show her the results of his surgery. "Not much call for a one-eared model."

She stopped chewing and leaned forward slightly. "It's not very noticeable unless you point it out—especially with your long hair. Couldn't they have done reconstructive surgery?"

He pushed his plate away, his appetite gone. He hated talking about this subject. "There was talk about that, but, honestly, after the treatments were over, I couldn't face another hospital room. And a few months later, my parents died within a week of each other. The result of a car accident. There was a lot to handle, estate-wise."

Her expressive face twisted in pain. "Oh, my God,

Rufus. That's too horrible. No wonder you walked into the woods and didn't come out." She reached across the table to squeeze his hand. "I'm so sorry."

He ran his thumb back and forth across her soft skin. "I don't talk about this because it sounds like a soap opera." He faked a smile. "I think I dated a woman who acted this very storyline."

She topped his thumb with her own and kept it pinned in place. "You don't have to pretend with me, Rufus. My father's death was a thousand times worse than my divorce. I can't imagine trying to deal with that kind of loss while you were recovering from cancer treatments."

Her empathy sounded authentic. It gave him the courage to say something he'd never admitted aloud. "My parents didn't come to New York for any of my treatments. Mom wasn't well. She'd developed a debilitating case of rheumatoid arthritis after Stephen died. Dad never left the ranch, except to attend high school basketball games. That's how it happened. They were on their way home from a game when the truck hit a patch of black ice."

"How awful. I suppose you had people telling you things like, 'At least, they went together.' "

He nodded. As lifelong residents of a small agricultural community, his parents' funerals had been over-flowing—even in the dead of winter. He'd heard all kinds of syrupy drivel intended to make him feel better. All any of it did was make Rufus feel more guilty.

One of the most popular was "Now, your parents will be with Stephen. Your dad was never the same after he died. And your poor mother missed him so."

"At my father's funeral, I remember a woman I'd never met before—one of Dad's dental patients, I think—tell me he was in a better place. I wanted to slap her. But Mom shook the lady's hand and smiled and thanked her for coming. I hated my mother so much that day. The pretense. The fake smiles."

He knew exactly what she meant. Especially the part about the pretense. There he was glad-handing mourners when it should have been him in the casket. He'd felt the same way at his brother's funeral a few years earlier and nothing had changed. Only his guilt had tripled.

He was about to change the subject by asking about her dad when she asked, "So, you're in remission, huh?"

"I guess you could say that."

She cocked her head, her coffee mug stopping partway to her lips. "What does your doctor say? Who do you see? Someone in Rapid?"

He stood, collecting both plates to carry to the sink. "I never got around to finding a local doctor. I figured as long as I eat right and stay out of the sun, I'll be okay."

"Pardon?" Her voice went high and squeaky—enough to make Rat-Girl bark. "You haven't done any follow-ups since you moved here? No blood work? Not even a PET scan to see if there's any activity?"

"No, but I feel great."

She jumped to her feet, sending the stool wobbling backward. The dogs scattered, their nails scratching against the tile floor like hail on the hood of a car.

Rufus turned to see Rachel stalk across the room, her expression furious. "You ass," she snapped.

"Huh?"

"You're a fool. A stupid, selfish fool. At the moment, I hate you more than I ever hated my stupid fool of a husband. He was small, petty and selfish. You are kind, generous and wonderful. If I didn't hate you, I'd love you. But I watched one man I loved die a slow and horrible death. I won't do that again for anybody."

She spun around, poised to dash away, but he stopped her. Inside his head, her words of accusation melded with his father's that night after his brother's fall. "Where were you, Rob? Flirting with a girl when you should have been watching your brother? You knew he'd do anything to impress you. If he dies, you only have yourself to blame. You and your damn ego."

"Wait. Let me explain." But what was there to say, really? He'd done everything the doctors ordered to beat the cancer because he had a mission he needed to see through to the end. Once his brother's legacy looked like a done deal, he'd carried on in peace and relative happiness. He'd pushed his health issue into a small, dark corner of his brain—not unlike the space in his Dreamhouses.

She looked at him, eyes shimmering with unshed tears. "Well?"

He let go of her arm.

"That's what I thought. I'm going home, now. I need to shower and change. I'll be back tomorrow, regular time, to process orders. I intend to honor our business deal…at least through the first of the year. But there can't be anything else between us. Personal stuff. Ever." She paused. "I can't pretend to understand why you'd put yourself at such risk. Maybe you don't think your life is worth living. But, trust me, dying isn't all that it's cracked up to be."

She petted each of the dogs on her way out, leaving Rufus with a sense of regret so bitter he couldn't taste the maple syrup he'd been eating. She'd changed his life in a matter of weeks, and now she was walking away. And he had no one to blame but himself. As usual.

CHAPTER FIFTEEN

RACHEL PAUSED ON THE stoop of Libby's house, dread and heartache robbing her of any joy she normally would have felt about attending her first meeting of the Wine, Women and Words Book Club. She'd fully intended to skip this get-together, but Kat wouldn't hear of it.

"You've read the book, which is more than some can say. You've been looking forward to this for weeks. You have to come. I don't know what's going on with you, Rae, but 'too tired' isn't an acceptable excuse. Not with these ladies. I'll see you there."

Rachel was tired, but not from not the exhaustion of hard work and physical effort. More the kind that comes from not being able to sleep and having every passionate moment of an affair that should never have happened rushing through her mind when she did manage to drift off.

"Damn," she muttered under her breath. Switching the bag in her right hand to her left, she knocked.

The chilly temperature made her breath crystallize in a fog. Her nose was cold and the fingertips in her gloves felt numb even from the very short walk to the main house from her cottage.

She tried the bell. A second later, the door jerked

open. "Rachel," a red-haired woman wearing a pretty cranberry-colored wool dress exclaimed. "I thought I heard a knock but everyone is talking. Sorry about that. Come in before you freeze."

Rachel had bumped in to Jenna Murphy several times over the past few days. Rachel found her to be an exuberant person with a lot on her plate, so to speak. In addition to writing scripts for *Sentinel Passtime,* she owned the Mystery Spot, a summer tourist enterprise that Rachel was hoping to pin down as a client.

"Hi," Rachel said, stomping off any extra snow on the mat inside the foyer. "Looks like it's definitely going to be a white Christmas, right?"

"For those of you staying here," she said, her tone obviously conflicted. "Shane and Mom twisted my arm to celebrate Christmas in California. We're gearing up to start shooting right after the first of the year, so it makes sense, but that will mean missing the wedding."

"Char told me that this morning," Rachel said, handing Jenna her bag so she could take off her jacket. "I was sorry to take your names off the list. But since you're hosting the newlyweds—and the boys—on the first part of their honeymoon, I'm sure that will make up for it."

Jenna pulled out the bottle of wine to read the label. "Ooh, we'll open this one first," she said with a wide grin. "Come on. Come on."

Rachel added her jacket to the others on the coatrack near the door and hurried to follow. Jenna stopped abruptly two steps later. "I forgot to mention the house," she said, turning to face her. "Kat and I were just talking. She said your mom is coming for the holidays and I sug-

gested she stay at my place. I have to keep the heat on
to prevent the pipes from freezing, so it seems a waste
to have it sit empty."

Rachel had been wrapped up in her recent case of
moping and she hadn't really given any thought to
where her mother would stay. "That's great, Jenna.
Thanks. Mom and me sharing my little house might
have led to some horrible headlines involving matricide
and mental breakdowns."

Jenna laughed. "I know exactly what you mean. Been
there, done that, as they say. Believe me, it really makes
all the difference in the world when your mother has a
life of her own."

The statement not only made sense, it made Rachel
wonder if retirement hadn't been a huge mistake where
her mother was concerned. Maybe Rosaline needed to
return to work.

"She's here," Jenna called, leading the way. "Our
newest victim, I mean, member."

An hour or so later, they still hadn't gotten around to
discussing the book. Apparently, diverse conversations
were not uncommon with this group.

Char had started things off by passing out photos
she'd taken at the holiday party in Lower Brule where
Eli, as Lakota Santa, had distributed the toys and books
he'd picked up at Libby's party.

"Next year, you all have to come, too. The food was
amazing and the kids were over-the-moon happy. I can't
tell you what a success this was."

That thread of chatter had led to recapping of the
gifting tree concept and how much money had been
raised for various charities. "Cooper gave me the final

list this morning," Libby said. "He was so proud. He wants everyone to have a copy so you can start planning your donations for next year."

Rachel's heart sped up as she scanned the sheet. Sure enough, Stephen's House was at the top of the list. She'd researched the organization online. A mother's devotion. A community's kindhearted generosity. A brother's hope that no family should have to choose between caring for a loved one and keeping a roof over their heads.

Rufus's story—or, rather, R. J. Milne's, as he was identified in the PR piece—brought her to tears. Every mile of that long drive to the hospital probably added to his sense of responsibility.

In the two days since their morning after chat, she'd seen him, of course, but he respected her edict to keep their conversations strictly about work. Even that contact had been difficult for her. She couldn't look at him in coveralls and plaid without picturing him in his designer suit. Or, better, naked. Her mouth went dry thinking about it.

Suddenly aware that the other members were looking at her as though she might have been asked something and failed to respond, she swallowed stiffly. "Huh?"

Libby chuckled. "Yep. You were right, Char." She looked around. "Love-struck."

"No question."

"Most definitely."

"Busted." The last came from Mac's fiancée, Morgana. "I told Mac at the party it was like watching *Beauty and the Beast* when the enchantment lifts and, suddenly, the beast is beautiful again." Her perfect skin turned a delicate rosy hue. "Can you tell I've been watching videos with Megan?"

Everyone laughed. The beautiful television star was dressed casually in jeans and a *Sentinel Passtime* sweatshirt, but there was no missing the sparkly diamond on her finger.

"We all fell a teeny bit in love with Rufus the other night, didn't we?" Kat said, reaching out to squeeze Rachel's arm. "And, believe me, Jack noticed and was very eager to impress me with his, uh, magic when we got home."

Char made a face. "T.M.I., as my son would say. Too much information."

Rachel wasn't planning to talk about what happened between her and Rufus. She wasn't the close girlfriend type. She had tons of friends, but none were true confidantes. Still, it was tempting to get another woman's perspective. She'd never felt more confused and conflicted.

"Rufus and I aren't speaking. Well, other than work stuff."

"Whoa," Char said. "You hit the skids awfully fast. Must be the holidays. Everyone gets a little crazy this time of year."

Rachel wasn't offended by her friend's candid assessment. Char was nothing if not frank.

"Every new relationship has its crash-and-burn moments," Morgana said. "I was absolutely positive Mac would never want to speak to me again after he found out the truth about my past. But we both worked through our issues. If you care about him, you owe it to yourself to try."

"What if the person you care about doesn't care enough about himself?"

"What do you mean?" Libby asked, her tone defensive. "Just because Rufus doesn't go to the barber regularly doesn't mean—"

"I don't give a damn about his hair," Rachel cut in, passionately. "I mean follow-up visits to a doctor. That's what you do if you've been diagnosed with and treated for cancer. You can't simply hide in the woods and hope you're cured. It doesn't work that way. I know. I watched my dad die from cancer, but it was the denial that killed him."

Libby blanched. "Rufus has cancer? What kind?"

"Melanoma. Before he moved here," she confessed, feeling guilty about sharing something private. She wondered if breaching this confidence might be one more nail in the coffin of their relationship. "I told you more than I should have. I'm sorry. He's a private person, and he has every right to make his own choices. I'm sure he didn't expect me to react the way I did, but—" She didn't complete the thought. She couldn't go through her rationale again—not when it brought memories she couldn't bear to think about. Her father's final days, the pain and indignity and fear.

"Maybe now would be a good time to talk about the book," Kat said, attempting to smile. "I know you all think I was crazy to pick such a sad book at this time in my life—two women brutalized by the same man they both had the sad misfortune to marry. But I was inspired by the love and compassion the two women grew to have for each other. That was beautiful, wasn't it?"

Rachel was grateful for the diversion and readily joined in the lively discussion. These women could be her friends, she sensed. And by the time they made one final toast—"May everyone we know and love find peace and joy this holiday season"—she felt almost whole.

"Even those of us who were foolish enough to set their wedding day between Christmas and New Year's," Kat murmured under her breath.

The conversation immediately switched to wedding plans as everyone pitched in to clean up. There was a short debate about whose turn it was to pick the next book and whether or not they should skip a month since Libby wasn't going to be able to travel until after the baby was born. In the end they decided on a title and tentative date.

"You'll come, won't you, Rachel?" Morgan asked.

"Most definitely." *If I haven't thrown in the towel and moved home with my mother.*

Not that she planned to give up, but breaking up with Rufus felt like the last straw. Proof that her mother was right. Rachel really couldn't read people, and she really did make the most awful choices for herself when it came to men.

Since Rachel lived the closest, she volunteered to load the dishwasher. She wished she was going home to the cabin where Rufus was probably still hard at work. But she wasn't. If he was in remission and the cancer came back, she'd support him. What she couldn't do was facilitate his denial.

"Do you think Rufus's cancer may have spread?" Libby asked when they were alone.

Rachel shook her head. "No. He seems healthy, but melanoma isn't easy to beat. I did a little research."

Libby folded a couple of extra napkins and put them away. "I'm sure you did. I'd want to know everything I could about the enemy that was trying to take away someone I loved."

Rachel didn't correct her friend's assumption. Rufus was worthy of loving, even if she couldn't bring herself to commit her heart.

"You know, Rachel, every life—and death—is different. I never gave that much thought until I lost Gran. But now I know that as hard as it is to watch someone you love die, that's the price you pay to be with them for as long as you can."

Libby's words stayed with her as Rachel gathered up her book and jacket and walked home. Watching her father's slow decline had been intense, brutal and emotionally devastating, but in a way that one-on-one time with him had been a gift. Something hers alone.

Libby was right. Love wasn't free. And relationships weren't easy. Rachel had married Trevor because he made it seem all fun and games and she'd been looking for an escape. But the cost to her pride and self-esteem had been too high.

Rufus was different. He didn't ask anything of her. He wasn't ill at the moment. And he certainly didn't need a caretaker. He was strong, vital, fiercely independent and loyal to the max. Look at his dedication to his late brother's legacy. But the moment she heard the word *cancer,* she'd split. Why?

She kicked a clump of snow, drawing some satisfaction as it exploded in a fine powdery mist. She'd blown it. Overreacted. Panicked. Not at his perceived fallibility, but because of what he made her feel. Sex she could write off as basic need or hormonal folly. But getting a glimpse of the human being behind the facade was something else.

"Run, little girl, run," her father had called when she was a child, chasing her older brother. At what point in her life had she starting taking that advice literally? She'd run from her marriage without even attempting counseling. She'd run from her job the first chance she got. She'd left Denver with barely a conscious thought of what awaited her in Sentinel Pass. And now, she was running away again. From Rufus—or from the feelings he made her feel?

He had cancer. Okay. If he mattered to her, she'd deal with it.

He had a past that she knew practically nothing about. So…who didn't? He had the ability to make her head spin with desire and lust and…yes, damn it, love. When she was in his arms, she lost control in a way that felt both liberating and empowering.

But that wasn't possible. Her mother had always maintained that true power came from self-control.

"Think, Rachel," she murmured softly as she walked the rest of the way to her little bungalow. "Think."

By the time she'd walked inside, she'd made up her mind. She was going to do whatever it took to survive Christmas. If that meant avoiding Rufus, so be it. She'd get the last of his orders in the mail then turn her focus on her family and the wedding. After the first of the year, she'd take a hard look at her life and her business. Everything had been so rushed when she left Denver, she hadn't even found the time to do a detailed budget and cost-benefit analysis.

"Enough of that laissez faire attitude," she muttered. "In business and in my personal life."

At least someone would be happy. Mom.

RUFUS GRABBED HIS MUG and took a large gulp.

"Crap," he sputtered a second later, leaning over the sink to spit out the leftover taste in his mouth.

Cold tea he could tolerate, cold coffee made him ill. And he'd been drinking coffee again because the smell of it reminded him of Rachel.

He bent and cupped some water from the faucet. Anger made his hand shake. He was royally pissed off. Not about the coffee, but that was part of it.

Rachel had left her mark and he couldn't escape it. Not in his house, where he found her hair tie, her pen, a sketch she'd made of some early version of his Web design. And certainly not in his shop, where she continued to work every day. Productive, efficient, self-contained.

It wasn't that she ignored him. She smiled pleasantly. She brought the dogs treats and lavished them with attention. But she made it clear she intended to keep her distance with him. And the fact that she could turn off her emotions so easily really burned. Because he couldn't.

She'd flounced in, turned his life upside down, then sashayed out as if the emotional connection they'd shared never happened. He would have hated her if he didn't love her.

He turned off the faucet and looked out the window. The morning sun sparkled on the newly fallen snow. He hoped it would be melted by the time he got to Rapid City, where he would probably find a swarm of last-minute holiday shoppers. He felt a little sick thinking about it, but he refused to give in to his agoraphobia. He'd lived in freaking New York City, for heaven's sake. He could handle the second largest city in South Dakota.

He had another objective, too. He planned to buy a

cell phone and call his ex-agent, Marianne. Something he'd put off for far too long. For the past few days he'd felt a nagging urge to reexamine what happened at the very end of his career. Not because he had any desire to return to his former life—even if that were possible— but certain questions haunted him. *Did I give up too easily? If I'd had the reconstructive surgery, would I have had a few more good years?*

He didn't know what Marianne would say. Maybe he simply needed to reassure himself that he'd done the right thing by leaving. One thing he could count on from Marianne was the cold, hard truth.

He rinsed his mug and turned it upside down on a towel. "Do you guys want out?"

To his surprise, when he started toward the front of the house—the entrance he commonly used—the sound of twelve paws following didn't happen. He looked over his shoulder and spotted all three dogs sitting by the back door—the door Rachel used when she brought them a little treat each morning on her way to the shop. A secret she didn't think he knew about.

"Sorry, guys. Today's Sunday," he told his pets. "She isn't coming. No mail. No reason to be here."

That sad fact hurt him a lot more than it did his dogs. In the week since their blowup, he'd thought of little else. He loved her. He'd fallen for her that first day at Char's shop. He'd denied his feelings for a huge host of reasons that hadn't much changed. He wasn't worthy of her. Forget the cancer, he was too ravaged by life to make a good mate. She was wise to end it when she did.

He knew that, but the facts didn't make him want her any less. He still craved her voice, her smell, her smile.

He'd tried to fill the void with work, and he'd been surprisingly successful. Maybe a lifetime of faking his emotions finally served him well. Every morning when Rachel arrived, she found a dozen new Dreamhouses to package up and mail.

Twelve a day. A quota he knew he couldn't sustain. His entire body ached, and his hands were so sore he could barely make a fist. But the cutoff date for taking orders was almost here. And her last report told him he'd already made enough money to finish furnishing Stephen's House.

"Orders will probably fall off after the holidays," she'd told him. "But you might find demand is still high enough to hire part-time office help."

He took that to mean she wouldn't be applying for the job. He was well aware of the fact that she'd stopped unpacking boxes of her personal items. He didn't know if that meant she'd changed her mind about opening her Web design business in Sentinel Pass or if she simply planned to find a new office.

So many questions he couldn't ask. Why? Because she'd made it clear the only way he could be a part of her life was by doing the one thing he abhorred. The day after his last chemotherapy infusion, when he'd been barfing his guts out, he'd promised himself he'd take whatever time surgery and chemotherapy had bought him and live it well—in harmony with nature and relative peace.

Did that make him a fool? Probably. But she was wrong about one thing. He wasn't in denial. He didn't believe he'd truly beat the big C. But he'd fought one battle…and won. For now.

Of course the smart thing would be to see a doctor

for regular checkups. But since he couldn't imagine mounting a second defensive, why bother? If his cancer came back, so be it. He would have accomplished what he set out to do. His brother's memory would live on.

That should have been enough. And it might have been…until he met Rachel.

He ran upstairs, dressed quickly and hurried to the front door to pull on his snow boots. The dogs were waiting, tails wagging. "Sorry, my friends, no dogs allowed in the stores."

Chumley cocked his head and let out a low growl. The other two immediately went ballistic, jumping at the door. Confused because he hadn't heard a car pull in, Rufus yanked open the door.

He couldn't say for sure which of them was more surprised—Rufus or Rosaline Treadwell. "Dogs, hush."

The barking stopped.

"Hello," he said, poking his head out to look around. "Where's your car?"

She pointed toward the shop. "Rachel told me you spent your days—and most of your nights—in your workshop. Since no one answered my knock, I left my car and walked up." She stomped her feet, which, to Rufus's surprise, were encased in honest-to-goodness boots.

As if reading his thoughts, she looked down and said, "My grandsons are taking me to a local ski resort this afternoon. I asked a friend to help me buy weather-appropriate clothing."

"Oh." Made sense. He gave her credit for trying. In fact, he never would have guessed she cared enough about Kat's sons to make an effort. Not based on the way she'd basically ignored them at Libby's holiday party.

"May I come in?"

He hesitated. "I was headed out myself. But my truck is parked beside the shop. We could talk as we walk."

"Okay."

He grabbed his gloves and keys and, after giving his dogs a quick pet on the head, closed the door.

"You didn't lock it," she said, pulling on her gloves.

"The dogs won't let anyone in."

"Except my daughter." A statement, not a question.

He made sure she didn't slip on the steps before he told her, "Rachel is always welcome here, but I'm not expecting her. She doesn't work on Sundays."

She stopped him with a hand on his arm. "Please. Wait. I know I owe you an apology. My son gave me quite an earful the other day on the phone. It was long overdue. My late husband had a tendency to spoil me. He deferred to my wishes and made our children follow suit. Rachel was the most acquiescent child until her father died. Since that time, we've butted heads constantly." She held up a gloved hand as if anticipating his protest. "Don't misunderstand. She's a wonderful daughter and one of the most genuinely caring people you'll ever meet. I know she loves me, but she's also very mad at me."

He was surprised by her candor. Shocked speechless, actually. They kept walking, but more slowly than before.

Rosaline sighed. "You heard a little of this the other night at the party. Believe me, it's not easy admitting you're an overbearing busybody. I should have learned my lesson where Trevor was concerned, but I didn't. I nearly made the same mistake again with you."

He didn't know exactly what she meant by that, but it hardly seemed relevant. "Rachel and I are not together," he said, hoping that would end their conversation. She seemed far more likeable than the witch she'd been the other night, but if he and Rachel were history, then he might as well go back to his life of isolation.

She surprised him further by throwing back her head and laughing. "Perhaps because she's moping around her little cottage and you're doing…well, frankly, not what I expected. I got the impression you never left this place."

She looked around as if seeing his home and shop for the first time.

"Even a hermit can find some use for a cell phone."

"Rachel said you were smart. I should have trusted her judgment. Again," she stressed. Instead of an accompanying sigh, she made a little sound that hinted at stifled emotion.

Good grief, he thought, *Genghis Khan cries?*

They'd reached the shop, so he quickly hustled her inside. "Suppose you tell me why you're here?" He said, crossing his arms to face her.

"I'm a terrible mother. I was a good wife. Maybe not great, but I loved my husband. More than my daughter knows. Rachel thought I abandoned him in his hour of need. What she didn't understand was I couldn't bear to watch him die. It killed me inside. If I'd been thinking straight, I would have bought stock in tissue companies becaused I went though so many boxes. Does that sound heartless to you?"

"No. But I don't understand why you're telling me this."

"Because I think my daughter is love with you, and

I'm afraid that unless you and I make peace, I will never see her again."

"That doesn't sound like Rachel. She's generous and forgiving."

"She gets that from her father. He had the biggest heart of any man you ever met. It nearly—no, it truly did ruin him. His generosity was his downfall, and I have to admit that I was angry about that for a long, long time. We forgave each other, of course, before he died, but I don't think Rachel believes that." She took a breath then admitted, "I wasn't at his side when he passed away."

Rufus suddenly had a picture of Rachel, alone, with her daddy when he stopped breathing. "Was she...was she there alone?"

"What?" Her eyes went wide. "Oh. No. The hospice nurses sent her from the room moments after calling me. They knew it wouldn't be long. I rushed home from the bank. I did try. But I was too late."

He and his father hadn't been able to make it to his brother's bedside in time, either. A swift, unexpected memory rocked him. The truck swerving, his father overcorrecting, the sensation of sliding backward in a ditch. They'd been shook up but, fortunately, the truck was still drivable. In the end, though, their race had proven fruitless because Stephen was gone.

He knew at that moment he had two choices. Tell her his history or keep it to himself—like usual. He looked at her, debating. Maybe if she didn't seem so darn vulnerable. He led her to a chair. "My brother died when I was in high school," he started. "If you want to compare failings, I have to warn you, I'll win."

They talked for a good half hour. She was a better

listener than he expected. "I know it's a cliché, Rufus, but bad things do happen to good people. My husband didn't deserve to have his business and reputation ruined by a greedy opportunist. He didn't deserve to get cancer. Do I believe the two are connected? Yes. That cloud of guilt and anguish that followed him for the last few years of his life killed him as surely as the physical disease."

She looked him in the eyes and said firmly, "You didn't cause your brother's fall."

The quick change of subject took him off guard. He answered more honestly than he might have if he'd had time to think about it. "I could have quit practice a few minutes early and made him go home with me."

"Guilt. When researchers find a cure for that, doctors might be treating a lot less cancer."

Rosaline checked her watch. "I have to go." She started to button her coat, which she hadn't removed. "I know that nothing I say is going to fix your issues, Rufus. But I will tell you what helped me carry on after my husband died. I reminded myself that he would have wanted me to be happy. He loved me that much. Don't you think your brother would have wanted that for you, too?"

He did. But there was so much more than simply Stephen's death to feel responsible for: his mother's chronic pain, his father's undiagnosed, untreated depression, the accident that took their lives. All because he'd been too busy doing his own thing to watch out for his brother, his best friend.

"Rachel doesn't know I came here," Rosaline said, standing up. "We haven't been talking much lately. I had to stop making suggestions about the wedding because she got so defensive. The holidays are never easy, and this one is going to be particularly tough. So many changes in such a short time."

He understood all too well. He felt the same.

As they walked to the door, she described the logistics of the upcoming week. Christmas then a wedding a few days later. He pictured Rachel skillfully juggling all the responsibilities that went with planning a wedding, welcoming three new members into the family at Christmas and dealing with his business.

Maybe now isn't the right time to do this. Maybe I should put it off until after the first of the year.

Rosaline coughed, letting him know she'd asked him something and he hadn't answered. "Sorry. What did you say?"

"I offered to call my friend's son. He's a top-tier oncologist in Florida. Specializes in skin cancer. Always busy, but I know he'd make time for you if I asked."

Her offer surprised him. "Thank you. I would consider him for a second opinion, if I need one. But I e-mailed my former doctor yesterday. He wants me to come to New York."

Her eyes went wide. "Have you told Rachel?"

"I'm not going to. If the screening turns out bad, I don't want her to know."

Rosaline looked at him shrewdly. "I won't tell her, but you obviously don't know my daughter very well. She might have stepped away when she thought you were being an idiot. But you could never keep her from fighting the good fight for someone she loves."

He believed her, but he loved her daughter too much to put her through that again. Better she never found out.

"Who's taking care of your dogs?"

He frowned. Calling a local vet to see about dog boarding was on his To-do list once he had a cell phone. "I'm working on that."

"Ask Rachel. Write her a note. I'll deliver it after you've left. That way you don't have to answer any questions."

His eyes narrowed suspiciously. "You won't tell her where I am and why?"

"I promise. This is between you and my daughter." She made a zipper sign across her mouth. "But I do think she deserves to hear the verdict—one way or the other. Don't you?"

Yes. He owed her that. Had the dragon stayed slain? They'd know soon enough.

CHAPTER SIXTEEN

"SO HOW DOES THIS WORK, doggies?" Rachel asked, softly kicking the side of the copper tub with the toe of her boot. "He slides the empty thing in front of the fire then fills it? Bucket-by-bucket?"

The time-consuming process made her hesitate... until she looked inside the pristine vessel and spotted a neatly coiled hose with an adaptor that obviously fit on the kitchen faucet. "Oh," she exclaimed, smiling. "Much better."

The idea of relaxing in a hot bath had been in her head all day. Today was Christmas Eve. She'd tidied up her office and Rufus's work space around noon then spent the rest of the day visiting friends, dropping off gifts and doing a few last-minute fixes in the teepee in preparation for the wedding. Like every day since her mother delivered Rufus's cryptic note, Rachel also spent a good deal of time worrying about him and questioning what she was doing sleeping in his bed when they obviously had no chance of coming together on common ground.

Especially after she gave in to her curiosity and checked his e-mail account where she found his airline itinerary to New York City. He'd gone back to his old life without telling her, without talking things over or even giving her any kind of warning. She didn't know what that meant, but her imagination had had a field day. Luckily, his dogs were good listeners, and at some point she'd stopped being mad.

Now, she was worried.

"I hope he's okay," she said, reaching out to ruffle Chumley's thick coat. The older dog groaned in appreciation. Chum and Rachel had bonded over a bowl of popcorn one night after the other dogs were asleep.

Rachel had never experienced quiet such as the kind that came with an isolated cabin in the middle of winter. No television. She hadn't been able to figure out his complicated stereo. No laptop—the Internet connection only worked at the shop. The fire, the animals and hints of Rufus…and his alter ego, R. J. Milne. She even had a few glimpses of the boy he'd been once upon a time. A handsome basketball player named Robin. Whose little brother, Stephen, was the team's mascot.

She stared into the swirling water and thought about what she'd learned so far. He'd been an average student but popular. She'd spotted his black-and-white image half a dozen times in a yearbook she found on his bookshelf. At first, she'd had a difficult time connecting Robin, or "Rob" as his friends wrote on inside jackets, to the haughty, disdainful face of a model named R. J. Milne.

She couldn't help but stare at his image—fully dressed or mostly naked. He was gorgeous. Physical perfection. Or close enough at first glance to make you think he was perfect. It wasn't until she grouped together all the shots that she saw how unhappy he was. Tortured, really. His eyes carried the empty, soulless stare of a prisoner of war.

"Woof."

Lost in thought, she startled at the sound, causing the water to spray everywhere. All three dogs scrambled to safety. She turned off the hose. "Thanks for the heads-up, Chum. I need to pay better attention. I don't want to flood the place when I get in."

She grabbed a towel from the adjoining bathroom. She'd already figured out that by attaching the same hose to the spigot at the bottom of the tub, she could discharge the water into some kind of receptacle under the house. Gray water, she vaguely remembered hearing Rufus say.

She put another log on the fire then stripped and quickly got into the tub. "Hot, hot, hot," she cried, slowly lowering herself into the water.

She kept an eye on the water level, making sure her body displacement didn't create a flood. "An inch to spare. Check that out, Chum," she said.

With a sigh of contentment, she sank back. She'd never been alone in such a large tub. A noisy, bubbling hot tub, of course, with Trevor and friends. But this was completely different.

Trevor's name reminded her. He'd called that morning and left a message on her voice mail. "Merry Christmas. I hope the New Year will be good to us both, Rae. I'm really sorry about how things turned out. I'm a world-class jerk and you deserve better."

She agreed. And hearing him admit that had been a sort of balm. It might have been what spurred her to call her mother and invite her to lunch. "I know you're busy, Mom, but we should talk."

"I agree, but I'm making Daneen's potato soup. She

claims it's the world's best and I can't risk letting it burn. Do you want to come here and be my taster?"

Here was Jenna's house—half a mile, at most, from Libby's place where Rachel would have been if she weren't dog-sitting for Rufus. But, still, the invitation was made, the white flag extended, how could she say no? "Sure. I'll see you in twenty minutes."

And to Rachel's surprise, none of her worst-case scenarios came to pass. "You seem different, Mom. What's going on?" she finally asked over a second helping of the best potato soup she'd ever tasted.

"I'm retired, Rachel. And not simply from the bank. A wise man pointed out to me that my work raising you and your brother was done. I did a good job, too, but now it's time to let you and Jack handle things. Amazing how liberating that kind of acknowledgment can be."

"No more second-guessing our decisions?"

"Have I called you even once this week about wedding plans?"

Rachel had to admit Mom hadn't. The only time they'd talked was when Mom delivered Rufus's note. Even then, she'd kept her comments to a minimum, saying, "I know nothing about his plans, only that he needs your help with his animals. I assured him that wouldn't be a problem."

Period. That had been it. No suggestions on how to handle the logistics of moving temporarily into Rufus's house. No offers to help ease Rachel's load by handling some of the wedding plans.

"I think everything is done," Rachel had said. "At least, until the actual day of the wedding. We should be able to relax and enjoy Christmas."

"Because you are an excellent planner, Rachel. I have no doubt that you are going to be successful in anything you choose to do."

Rachel had been touched. She'd hugged her mother then hurried off to finish her other errands, promising to return early enough to play games with Jordie and Tag.

Jack, Kat and the boys had shown up minutes after Rachel returned. They'd feasted on soup, toasted with wine and each opened one present. The boys opened Rosaline's gift to them—a new Wii. In the morning, they'd get the two games Rachel bought.

While Jack helped Tag link the control box to Jenna's TV, Mom had handed Rachel a gift to open.

A gorgeous, sexy peignoir. The robe was plum-colored satin, the gown simple but elegant with cleverly positioned panels of lace. The over-the-top high-heel slippers were straight out of the 1950s with feathery pom-poms.

The dogs had sniffed the shoes suspiciously when Rachel returned home around midnight.

She shifted one leg languidly, trying to picture Rufus's reaction to her modeling her new gift for him. A shiver of desire passed through her body. She missed him. Sleeping in his bed every night smelling his scent on the sheets had only made her want him more. If he didn't come back soon…she didn't know how to finish the thought. She had so many unanswered questions.

Heaving a long, bone-deep sigh, she fished around the bottom of the tub for the slim bar of soap she'd tossed in earlier. She made an effort to keep her splashing to a minimum as she lathered and rinsed. Then she stood and copied what she'd seen Rufus do that morning when she played the voyeur.

One leg, one foot. Hop over the side of the tub to repeat the opposite limb. Then she dried the rest of her body and tossed the damp towel on the floor in front of the fire. Shivering despite the room's pleasant warmth, she slipped on her new gown. The material was decadently rich and seductive. The lace slanted diagonally across her nipples. This was not a nightgown meant to be worn alone.

"Well, Santa's gonna get an eyeful," she told the dogs. "Because I'm wearing this to bed."

She wormed her feet into the silly slippers then did a clumsy pirouette. Rat-Girl barked, attacking Rachel's feet when she started toward the kitchen. "Rat, please. You're going to trip me. Settle down and you can all share my cocoa." She frowned. "I'll pour three bowls of warm milk before I add the chocolate. Okay?"

She didn't know if the promise of a treat was all it took to diffuse the little dog's hatred of the puffy shoes, but Rat did quit barking. Fred followed, too. Chumley remained by the door.

"Poor Chum," Rachel called. "Still think Santa's going to deliver your master in his magic sleigh, huh?"

The dog didn't answer. Probably because that was Rachel's fantasy, not Chumley's. And when Chumley did bark a few minutes later, Rachel assumed it was in response to the wind banging the storm door, like usual. It had taken her a couple of nights to get used to the sounds this house made, but slowly the place began to feel like home.

She didn't know if that was a good thing or the worst that could possibly happen. She wouldn't know the answer until Rufus returned.

CHAPTER SEVENTEEN

RUFUS SPOTTED THE TUB the moment he stepped on the porch. He gave her credit for taking on the task. Lugging the clumsy thing from the storage closet and connecting the hose took some effort.

He craned his neck but didn't see any sign of her in the tub. He didn't see his dogs, either. Until he tried the door handle.

"Woof."

Chumley.

Rufus juggled his key ring to find the house key he very rarely used. He wasn't surprised Rachel had chosen to take precautions.

Only one dog was there to greet him. Chumley's broad tail flashed back and forth with obvious happiness. "Hello, friend," he said softly, going down on one knee to give the dog a hug. "Yes, I brought you a treat, but you have to wait for the others. Where are they?"

He shrugged off his jacket and tossed it over the hook beside the door. He was relieved to see Rachel's puffy jacket. He knew he should have called to give her a heads-up about his return, but he was afraid she might leave. And he had so much he wanted to tell her.

He set down his carry-on bag and carefully unzipped

it. Good thing he was a light traveler, because he'd done the unthinkable at Chicago's O'Hare airport. On Christmas Eve day, in the midst of holiday travel mayhem, he'd gone shopping. Small things, obviously, but gifts that made him feel more alive than any edict from his doctor.

One of the paper sacks was adorned with paw prints. Chumley's nose twitched. "Not yet, pal. It isn't quite midnight."

He stood and headed toward the sounds coming from the kitchen. He found Rachel—in a gorgeous peignoir—standing before his stove, leaning over to waft the steam from whatever was cooking toward her nose. In a manner very much like Chumley, she sniffed the air. "Oooh, yum."

As she rocked back on her ridiculously sexy stilettos, she happened to glance sideways. Half a second later, she let out a small, high-pitched shriek and pitched the wooden spoon she was holding straight at his head.

Rufus ducked in time. Fred and Rat-Girl, following the action and probably sensing Rachel's fear, started barking with equal parts joy and apprehension. He leaned down to calm them. "Sorry. Sorry. I didn't mean to scare you. I should have coughed or something."

Rachel had staggered backward before catching her balance by grabbing the counter. Chest heaving from panic, she couldn't have looked sexier if she'd been staged by the best film noir art director in New York.

His mouth went dry and everything he'd planned to say—and rehearsed on the drive from the airport—flew out of his mind. He dropped the bags on the island as he cleared the distance between them. He crushed her to him, kissing her fast and hard before she could speak.

Her arms closed around his neck after the tiniest hesitation. She kissed him back, matching his need and hunger. Hope blossomed inside him. Maybe, just maybe, she'd forgive him.

When he finally eased back to catch his breath and give them both a moment, he rested his forehead against hers and said, "I mean it, Rachel. I'm sorry. For everything."

Her fingers continued to touch and stroke the hair at the back of his neck. He'd visited his favorite stylist when he was in New York. A man whose skill with scissors had made him a legend. "I'm keeping the length but giving you a face again, you hairy beast," Troy had said with his usual over-the-top delivery. "And if I ever see you with a beard, I'll sedate you and shave your head. This face—imperfect ear and all—is too real, too relevant for facial hair."

Rufus didn't know exactly what Troy meant, but he took the man at his word. No more beard. He was done hiding. His elaborate coping mechanism hadn't worked. The world—Rachel, at least—had found him and there was no going back.

Nor did he want to. Even if she couldn't forgive him or was too put off by his health issues to risk getting involved with him, long-term.

"You don't know how badly I want to carry you off to my lair and make love to you," he said. "You're beautiful. Gorgeous. Beyond sexy. Is this new?"

She nodded. "Christmas present from my mother." He could tell she was trying to keep her hurt feelings from showing. He'd disappeared with only a short note asking her to handle everything in his absence. A few days before Christmas. She had every right to be mad, upset, bruised. But she was gamely trying to fake it. "How was your trip?"

He took a deep breath and stepped back. "Come into the living room and I'll tell you all about it."

He reached for her hand, but she made a gasping sound and pointed to the stove. "I might have scalded my cocoa."

"Probably not the only thing of mine you would have liked to scald recently," he said, giving her room to move around.

"You've got that right," she muttered under her breath. But to his face, she said, "This isn't your cocoa. It's mine. Part of a chocolate gift basket from Char and Eli. All the book club members got one. But I'll share. Let me add some more milk to the pan."

He turned off the knob. "Later. I slept a little bit on the plane, but the time change will probably catch up with me soon. Can we talk while I'm still making sense?"

She nodded and sashayed ahead of him into the living room. Watching her hips undulate in the much too sexy heels made the blood leave his brain for a second or two, but he forced himself to stay focused on what he had to say. She stopped suddenly.

"Oh, nuts. I forgot about the tub."

"No problem. I leave it out overnight sometimes to put moisture in the air. It's fine."

He could tell she didn't believe his lie, but he didn't want to talk about bathtubs. Not when it was tempting to refill this one with hot water and share it with her.

"So…where did you go?" she asked.

"New York. I told the oncologist who treated me the first time that it was an emergency. He was expecting to see me on my death bed, but once he got over being pissed off at me, he agreed to give me a full exam. CT scan, MRI, PET."

She pulled a decorative couch pillow that had been his mother's into her lap. "Can you tell me what it showed?"

He made a goose egg with his thumb and fingers. "Zero activity. No mets—that's short for metastases in any area. And they did an MRI of the brain to be sure it hadn't spread to my head. Nothing there, either. Cancer, I mean."

She smiled at his little joke but a second later her smile grew until she was grinning like a small sun. "That's wonderful news, Rufus. I'm so happy for you."

He didn't like the sound of that. Going to the doctor hadn't been for him alone. He'd done it for her, too. For them.

"While I was there, I met my former agent, Marianne Diminici, for lunch." At the Plaza, their favorite old haunt. Not much had changed since he'd last been there—only the faces of the exposure-hungry models and the overplayed ennui of the booking agents. She'd set him straight about a couple of things.

"She told me about all the changes in the market."

"I must be getting old, Rob," Marianne had said. She'd been the one to insist he use his initials professionally, but, she'd always called him by his family nickname. "Frankly, I'm offended when you put a half-dressed model on a bucking machine and make her maul down a drippy, icky hamburger like it's some guy's you-know-what. There's looking sexy like you did in all of your ads, whether you were wearing a Brooks Brothers suit or a pair of Calvin Klein jockey shorts, then there's acting lewd and suggestive. Something is very broken. You were smart to get out when you did."

He'd laughed at that. "Ahem. If I remember correctly, you kicked me out on my still fairly sexy butt."

She'd sighed heavily and tossed down the dregs of her second cosmopolitan. "You were damaged goods, sweet cheeks. Emotionally damaged is one thing. The camera loves angst. But nobody wants to airbrush the missing half of an ear. I didn't think you could handle the rejection one casting agent at a time."

"So, you fired me to save me pain?"

"Exactly. Besides, your heart hadn't been in the work for a long time. I think you'd done your penance and were ready to move on. Cancer was the push you needed to change things."

As he'd thought about that comment on the flight home, he'd admitted she was right. Maybe not for the reasons she thought, but he had been sick of his life.

"Marianne told me I was never cut out for modeling. She said she saw my 'artist's soul.'" He made air quotes to make sure Rachel knew those weren't his words. "Most models show up, hit their mark and give the photographer whatever emotion the A.D. calls for. But it's Marianne's theory that I was learning from the staging process. Finding my inner artist."

"Was she right?"

He shrugged. "Who knows? But she cut me loose at a time when I didn't have the slightest idea what to do with my life. Sink or swim. I was pretty ticked off about that for a few years. I thought she was heartless."

"But now you're thinking she was a mama bird pushing you out of your comfort zone—no parachute attached?"

"Exactly. My mother wouldn't have done that. I left home—hell, I ran away—because I couldn't stand to hang around and watch my family implode from the grief of my brother's death. I had no plan, no goals. My driving need was to dull the pain. I fell into modeling and got swept up in the lifestyle. It wasn't a healthy lifestyle for me. As Marianne said, the cancer might have saved my life."

She seemed to be having trouble getting her mind around the idea.

"Rachel, before my brother died, my mom used to say things happen for a reason. I never heard her say that after his death. Probably because none of us could imagine why something that awful had to happen. But, in hindsight, I do think getting sick saved me. Having your career rug pulled out from under you can be liberating. I had enough money to do anything I wanted— even hide out from life."

She slowly nodded. "I guess that's what happened to me, too. Filing for a divorce and getting fired in quick succession is pretty harrowing. I spent a good deal of time under a mountain of covers."

He reached out and took her hand. He brought it to his lips. "Somehow that strange and awful combination of fate—or bad luck—made it possible for us to meet, and, believe me, you were worth the wait."

She swallowed. "What does that mean?"

"It means I love you. And I bought you a present. It must be after midnight, right?" He jumped to his feet and dashed to the kitchen. When he returned, he sat beside her and handed her a bag. The others he set on the floor. "Sorry it's not wrapped. If I'd had time, I would have gone to Tiffany's."

Her eyes went wide. Fear? Panic?

"Don't worry," he told her, his heart sinking a little. "It's not an engagement ring. I think that kind of thing requires a bit more forethought and the woman's input. I bought this between planes at O'Hare."

She relaxed visibly and reached into the bag. After tugging free the tissue paper, she held a jeweler's box on the palm of her outstretched hand. "Are you sure…?"

"Open it."

Inside, she found a pair of diamond earrings. Emerald cut. Huge. Gorgeous. "Holy smokes," she cried. "These had to cost a small fortune."

He turned up his hands. "They're beautiful, like you. And I also met with another old friend when I was in the city. He was my financial advisor before I got greedy and invested with you-know-who. Turns out I'm not quite as broke as I thought. I'd given him power of attorney over a portion of my investment portfolio before I had surgery. He undid a bunch of my mistakes and moved some of my holdings into a separate account. He told me every dime—less his fees, of course—has been sitting in a bank waiting for me to come to my senses."

Her mouth dropped open. "A friend indeed. That's wonderful. Then…you don't have to make Dream-houses anymore?"

"That's right. I don't."

Her expressive face fell but she faked a smile. "Great."

"I don't *have* to make them, but I plan to keep doing it anyway. Because being an artist is part of who I am."

"Really? You're not going back to New York?"

"I am…once a year. For a complete checkup. And my doctor is setting up quarterly blood screenings that I can do locally. But am I moving there? Hell, no. The noise.

Good Lord, I nearly lost my mind." He pulled her close. "My life is here. With you…I hope." He kissed her tenderly. "Consider those earrings a bribe. Can you forgive me for being such a jerk?"

She didn't answer right away. He didn't blame her, but he knew the only gift he wanted for Christmas was her love.

Rachel couldn't answer because she was struggling to remember even one of the complaints on her long list of grievances. Maybe she was distracted by the sparkle of the jewels winking so coyly at her, begging her to put them on. *They would look great with my nightie. Perfect. Could Mom have…?*

Her chief complaint popped into her head. "You left without saying goodbye. Again. That's twice now."

"I know. But your mother gave you my letter, obviously. You're here. She said you'd understand."

"Well, she was wrong. I didn't. I don't. I'm not good with surprises, Rufus. And, so far in our short acquaintance, you've sprung quite a few on me." She used her fingers to count. "Your name isn't—or wasn't—Rufus Miller. You're not a yeti-slash-hut-dwelling hermit. You had—have—this whole life—a big, glamorous existence that sounds a lot like the world I hated when I was married. And, then there's the whole denial about your health thing."

"But, in my own way, I was being proactive about my health, Rachel. My doctor gave me two thumbs up for my Spartan diet and healthy lifestyle. He said there are studies showing the link between cancer and stress." He made a global gesture. "You can't get much more stress-free than this, right?"

She knew that. Unfortunately, the knowledge only added to her fears. "But the past few weeks you've been working ten hours a day. I know you haven't been sleeping. I blame myself for this." She reached out and grabbed his arm. "If your cancer comes back, it might be my fault."

And I won't be able to fix it. I tried with Daddy and failed.

He embraced her. "Rachel, hard work doesn't make you sick. Not if you have happy stuff in your life to balance it out. I thought I was doing the right thing for my health, but it wasn't until you came into my life that I realized how empty my world was."

She heard the truth in his voice. "Really?"

"Oh, sweetheart, the day that box of sex toys exploded in my front yard will remain one of my best memories until the day I die. Many, many years from now, if you promise to be a part of my life."

That sounded a lot like a proposal. She waited several heartbeats, but one didn't follow. She was a little let down even though her rational brain told her she wasn't in a good place, emotionally, to think about remarrying. For heaven's sake, she silently scolded herself, the ink was barely dry on her divorce papers.

She tried to keep her tone flat as she asked, "As your Web designer?"

His chuckle was low and deep and deliciously inclusive. "No, silly. As my partner. Some interesting opportunities have come up, thanks to a bit of that social networking stuff you're so fond of. Although, I did it the old-fashioned way, face-to-face."

She punched him playfully and snatched up her

jeweler's box. "That sounds interesting," she said, quickly putting in her new earrings. "What kind of business opportunities?"

He took her jaw gently between his wonderfully roughened fingers, turning her chin to study her new sparklies. "Beautiful," he murmured before kissing her.

She resisted the urge to crawl into the warm sanctuary of his arms. "Business?" she asked, suddenly hearing her mother's voice.

Before she could take back the question, he answered, "I want to build more places like Stephen's House in towns and cities around the country."

Not at all what she had expected. "Won't that take a lot of money? How—"

He cut her off with another kiss. "Like I said, money isn't going to be a problem. I promise I'll tell you all about it in the morning, okay? Right now, I need to go to bed." He stifled a yawn. "The time difference is catching up with me."

She felt instantly contrite. "Oh, sure. Of course. It's ghastly late. Do you want me to go?"

He blinked, eyes wide open. "What? No. I want you to stay. Do you want to stay?"

She nodded. "Yeah. I do. I'm sorry if I'm not quite up to speed. I'm a little wiped out, too. My mom hosted dinner tonight. She's house-sitting for Jenna. It was good. But I had a lot of last-minute wedding things to handle today, too. I'm not making a lot of sense, am I?"

He put his arm around her shoulders. "No. It's me. I might have used up all my social graces in the city. I've reverted back to my old self. Yeti man no talk pretty," he joked. "But yeti man kiss good, huh?"

She nodded. "Oh, yeah. Very good." She pressed her lips to his to prove how much she liked his kisses.

He was the one to pull back. "We go kiss now," he said, staring deep into her eyes. "In bed." He pointed upward. "Okay?"

The last was in his real voice. No more teasing. He was asking her to stay the night with him.

The old Rachel would have demanded answers, a more concrete agenda. Her mother would have wanted everything in writing. But rational thought disappeared the moment he deepened his kiss. His taste was so familiar and reassuring. His hand touching her breast brought to life every bit of the passion she'd imagined while sleeping in his bed.

"Upstairs," she demanded. "Now."

He stood and pulled her to her feet. As they headed toward the staircase, Rachel suddenly remembered something she'd planned to give him…if the timing was right and she was brave enough. "Wait. One minute. I have something for you, too." She felt herself blush, but, fortunately, Rufus was distracted by the dogs. As he petted each one and praised them and told them good-night, she sprinted to the coat closet and grabbed the large, festive Rudolph gift bag she'd impulsively bought after her talk with Libby.

She'd made up her mind to "live forward without regrets"—until her mother handed her Rufus's note asking Rachel to dog-sit while he mysteriously disappeared. At that moment all her insecurities rode back on a big old wave of self-doubt. She'd hidden the bag in the closet, intending to take it home with her once he returned.

"What's that?" Rufus asked, looking over his shoulder as he led the way up the winding staircase.

"Oh, just a, uh, gag gift. Sorta." She fumbled with the Push Here button near Rudolph's ear. A second later his big red nose lit up and a tinny version of "Rudolph the Red-Nose Reindeer" started to play.

Rufus's chuckle gave her the courage she needed to hand it to him once they reached the second floor. "It's not your real present," she said. "That's on your workbench. I wasn't certain I'd see you, and figured you'd… Well, you can get it tomorrow." She glanced at the bedside clock. "Today. Merry Christmas."

He smiled. "Thank you. Can I open this now?"

"Okay."

His eyebrows were tweaked in obvious confusion, but he sat on the bed and carefully undid the ribbon she'd tied to hold the two plastic handles together. He pulled out handfuls of red-and-green tissue paper then looked inside.

His eyebrows shot up. "Oh. Cool. Why do these look familiar?" Then suddenly he burst out laughing. "You're re-gifting your sex toys. To me." His obvious glee made everything better. He got the joke. "This is awesome."

He also got the symbolism behind the gift. She hadn't trusted Trevor's love enough to play and laugh and risk feeling foolish or silly or exposed. She trusted Rufus.

"This is going to be fun."

She heaved a sigh of relief. And joy. She loved him, too, and couldn't wait to show him. "But hold on," he said, pawing through the bag. "There's nothing with feathers in here. You don't trust me with a whip?"

She slipped off her robe. "I trust you with my life,

and my future. You'll have to ask Fred about the whip in the morning. Seems he has a bit of a feather fetish."

"The dog," Rufus murmured. But she could tell he wasn't thinking about his pets or whips or anything else but her as she dropped the spaghetti straps of her sexy satin gown and slowly peeled down the fabric.

When she was standing before him, stark naked except for her stiletto heels, she wet her lips and said, "So...see anything you'd like to try first?"

"You," he answered with an impressive yeti growl. He pushed the gift bag aside and reached for her. She heard it topple to the floor. Once again, the ground was littered with mementos of her former life, but this time she wasn't mortified or embarrassed. They might even use one or two of the items. Sometime. Later.

Right now was about healing and reconnecting. And passion, of course.

CHAPTER EIGHTEEN

RUFUS'S EXHAUSTION disappeared in a heartbeat. He'd never seen anyone or anything as beautiful as the naked woman standing within arms' reach. She was the ultimate gift. "You are art perfected," he told her, running the backs of his fingertips along the curve of her belly.

He grasped the meaning behind the objects in the gift bag and knew what courage it took to give them to him. The gesture solidified his love for her in a way she couldn't possibly have guessed.

Trust was the biggie. The thing he'd lost when his brother died and his father blamed him. He hadn't trusted himself for years. But Rachel did. And that healed him better than any cancer treatment on the market.

He very lightly coaxed her closer with the tips of his fingers pressed against her waist. She wobbled a step, the heel of her shoe snagging the carpet. She put her hands on his shoulders to keep from falling into him. Her breasts were within reach of his lips and tongue, so he tasted and teased.

She squirmed with obvious pleasure, her grip on his shoulders tightening. He held her still with his hands splayed across her back as he buried his face between her breasts, rubbing back and forth to inhale her scent. She let out a tiny peep.

He looked up. "Am I hurting you?"

She laid her palm against his cheek. "I miss your beard. It was soft and tickled a little bit."

"Sorry," he apologized. "But it'll grow back."

"Promise?"

He nodded.

She ran her hands through his hair. "And this, too? I liked it longer."

"Women," he joked. "Never satisfied."

She turned sideways and settled her bare derriere on his knee. Crossing one leg over the other, provocatively, she made a sexy moue. "Oh, I think you'll be able to satisfy me." She touched her breast, making the nipple harden. "In fact, I'm sure of it."

His throat was too dry to swallow, but he did manage to kiss her. Her tongue met his in a dance that made all his juices flow. "Undress me. Quick. Before I die of needing you."

The gleam in her eyes said she liked the sound of that. The needing, not the dying. She deftly unbuttoned his shirt. He did the cuffs then yanked it off. She helped him peel up his undershirt, pausing only to lean down and lick his nipples while he fought free of it overhead.

His pants were tougher. She had to move. Which she did in the sexiest way possible, dropping to all fours and crawling, pantherlike, to the head of the bed, where she stretched out. Still wearing her puffy, glamour-girl heels.

He fumbled with his belt buckle, his fingers as sensitive as sausages. The zipper got stuck because it was crowded out by his fully engorged penis. He sucked in his gut and tugged downward. Finally. He dropped his pants, bikini briefs, too.

She'd been watching him, head resting on her upraised palm. "Not particularly graceful, but I'll give you full marks for not pinching your package in the zipper."

"Thanks. But I'm pretty sure even a little pain wouldn't have been able to dampen my ardor. I've missed you, Rachel Grey."

"Me, too," she admitted. "This is a great bed, but it's way too big and lonely without you. Come here, you."

He wanted to play more, tease her breathlessness, watch her come, but neither had the patience. He felt the urgency in her touch, in the way she took him in her hand. "I missed this part of you, especially. You've ruined me for other men, Rufus."

If he could have spoken, he would have told her the feeling was mutual, but all he could do was follow her lead. Still on her side, she looped one leg over him. Maybe her high heels changed the angle an incalculable fraction. Or maybe it was the long nights missing her. Whatever the reason, one thrust as he entered her brought a gasp of pleasure that set off quivers of excitement through both their bodies. He closed his eyes and strained for control but within seconds his need overtook him, too.

Surprised and a little embarrassed, he lifted his head and looked at her. "I— That was— Sorry."

"It was the shoes," she said, laughing. "Don't tell my mother."

She kicked off the silly shoes and maneuvered around until she was lying prone on top of him. His still partially erect penis was flexible and cooperative enough to fit back inside her. "That was one of the best, and by far the fastest orgasms I've ever experienced. Can we do that again?"

He shifted his hips under her, feeling definite interest from the part most needed to participate. "Maybe."

She sat up, wiggling her hips provocatively. "Good. Because you know what they say? Every time a woman has an orgasm on Christmas, an angel gets her wings."

Her tone was serious, but the naughty glint of humor in her eyes made him laugh. He was home. He was in love. And this was the best Christmas of his life. He only hoped she would still be smiling when he told her about his plans. In the morning. First, he needed sex and sleep. In that order.

"YOU BOUGHT THE BOYS presents, didn't you?" Rachel asked the moment Rufus joined her in the kitchen. She'd gotten up half an hour earlier. Rufus hadn't moved a muscle since about two o'clock when they both collapsed in satiated exhaustion after a record-setting triathlon of sex. She'd showered, dressed in her midnight blue velour lounging pants, matching snowflake top and wool-lined slippers.

After tiptoeing downstairs, she'd let the dogs out and made coffee. She'd tried to avoid peeking in the bags he'd left on the counter, but she didn't have the willpower. The gifts were amazingly astute and thoughtful.

"I did. Good morning to you, too. And merry Christmas. Where are the dogs? I bought them presents, as well."

"They're outside doing their morning ablutions. How'd you know what games to buy?"

"There were a couple of kids in the store about the same ages as Tag and Jordie. I asked their advice." He poured himself a cup of coffee, adding her favorite creamer. He stirred it absently then startled when he noticed her interest. "I'm hooked again. It's your fault. Coffee reminds me of you."

She liked that.

A familiar whine caught their attention. Rufus opened the kitchen door to three wet, snowy animals. She loved watching him interact with the dogs. It was how he'd be as a father, she realized. Patient, loving and consistent. She hadn't wanted to even think about kids when she was married to Trevor. But she did now.

She unconsciously rubbed her arm where the birth control implant was located. Maybe the time together without a child was something they needed as a couple. She'd made the mistake before of rushing too fast in a relationship. She wasn't going to do that again.

"What time do we have to be at your brother's?"

She looked at the clock above the sink. "Not for hours, yet. Kat wanted them to open gifts alone this morning. I think Mom was a little hurt, but Kat explained that neither of her parents was going to be there, either, then Mom felt better."

"Call her up. Have her come over for breakfast."

"Seriously?"

Rufus took a drink of coffee then walked to where she was sitting at the counter. "I like your mother. She's frank and honest. I need people like that in my life. When I was a celeb—" He held up his thumb and forefinger to show a tiny space. "I experienced a little bit of that obsequious reverence. It's seductive. It makes you do stupid things that you know are bad for you."

"How'd you manage to give it up?"

He shook his head and pointed to his ear. Hardly noticeable to her, but she could imagine how someone demanding perfection might be put off by it. "As Marianne said, it sometimes takes a wake-up call of major proportions to make you do the right thing."

"What else did your agent say?"

He grinned. "I'm glad you asked. I was too busy—" he gave her an impressive leer that made her knees weak "—last night to get into it, but Marianne said she knew a man who could turn my Dreamhouses into the next Chia Pet. If I wanted to go that way."

"Do you?"

"I don't know. It would commercialize the design. The originals would go up in value, I think. But I'd probably be asked to give up my rights. That would be tough. I like putting a little piece of myself in each Dreamhouse."

He sighed and shook his head. "But, like I said, the money could go to building places like Stephen's House—honoring the memory of Stephan Appelman Milne—all around the country. Denver, for instance. We could name it after your father."

She was touched. Her mother would be, too. Still, he was right. Handing over his design would pretty much close down their operation. "What would you do if you sold it?"

He shrugged. "Walk in the woods until I tripped over the next great inspiration?"

She waited, sensing there was more.

"Or, maybe I could surround myself with other creative people and see what happens." He looked down. "This probably makes me sound like some kind of altruistic hippie, but I got the idea from this flyer. It came in the mail the day I left for New York. Look."

He pulled a glossy, tri-fold promotional flyer heralding the impending grand opening of Stephen's House from the only messy drawer in the house. His junk drawer. He fumbled to open it, his hurry making him clumsy. She took it from him and laid it flat between them.

"There," he said, pointing to one of the photographs. "This is the first guest room they were able to finish."

She studied the image. Neat, homey and probably a sight for sore eyes to someone whose life had been turned upside down by trauma. But the two beds, small table and lamp in the photo were nothing extraordinary.

She looked up.

He tapped again. "The quilt on the wall. That was Mom's. She won prizes at the state fair and stuff. She made that quilt for Stephen a year or so before he died."

"Oh," she said, wishing she could have known these people who meant so much to Rufus. "It's really pretty. I've never seen anything like it. Now I know where you get your creative side."

She could tell he liked that. "I remember her working in the basement at night. And once a week, her quilting club would come over. I was too cool to spend much time around them, but they were amazing. And Mom said being in a group like that fired a person up. You fed off each other's creative energy."

"You're thinking about starting an artist's co-op?"

His grin was brighter than the morning sunlight streaming through the window. "My shop is a pretty good size. Maybe we could offer classes for people like me who don't think they're artists. Experiment with different mediums. We could teach each other." The sparkle in his eyes told her he could see his idea unfolding in his mind.

"I've always wanted to try throwing pots," he added, as if the idea were slightly embarrassing. "Maybe we could build a kiln."

Rachel was as moved by his passion and enthusiasm as she was by the possibilities. "I bet some of Char's artists would be happy to teach classes. Like Carl Tanninger, the guy who makes those fabulous Native American spears."

Rufus nodded enthusiastically. "But what we'd really need to make it a success is someone brilliant and dynamic who could then build us a Web site to sell our treasures."

"You think I'm brilliant?"

"I know you are. With you handling the Web sales everyone in our artists' workshop will be rich."

She doubted that, but she'd already proven with Rufus's site that she could generate an interest in the work that wouldn't happen if it was merely on display in a local gallery. "What makes you think there are other fledgling artists in the area who are looking for something like this?"

"Gut feeling," he said, tapping his hard, flat tummy. "Our mailman has been acting pretty curious about what we're shipping to all parts of the country. The other day he mentioned winning some kind of prize for a photograph he took. And I thought I picked up some thwarted artist vibes from the town gossip, too. What's her name?"

Rachel half choked on her sip of coffee. "You mean the grouchy lady at the civic center? Seriously?"

"Maybe. Put a paintbrush in the right person's hand

and who knows what will happen? I certainly didn't think of myself as an artist when I moved here. And if not for a little talent and a little luck, I never would have met you."

"Speaking of you and me, do I still have to pay you to go to the wedding with me?"

His laugh was rock solid and joyous. "How 'bout I take it out in trade?"

She pretended to think a moment. "Well…okay. I think that can be arranged."

They shared a moment of contented silence, then Rachel thought of another request she needed to ask. "Are you sure you're okay about going to Jack's today? People will make assumptions about us. There will be questions you might not be ready to answer." From her mother, for sure.

He pretended to debate the question. But only for a moment. He was through hiding out, and that meant interacting with Rachel's family—no matter how unhappy that might make her mother. "You bet I'm going. I plan to try my hand at a couple of these Wii games," he teased. "And next year, we'll host the festivities here."

"Next year." Her rueful smile said, "We'll see about that."

He walked to where she was standing and put his hands on her shoulders. "I know I came off as the kind of guy who didn't welcome change, but, guess what? A lot of things have changed. For the better, I might add. Thank you, Rachel."

"For what?"

"For rescuing me."

"Some people—my mom, for instance—might say

I threw you under the wheels of an oncoming train called life." She grinned. "But I did it for your own good," she added. "And mine."

"I agree. That's why I plan—when the moment's right—to ask you to marry me. Last night would have seemed too impetuous. We're better than that."

"We are?"

He nodded. "That kind of thing requires forethought and planning. A romantic setting. When it's just the two of us." He nodded toward the dogs and grinned. "And, most importantly, after you've put your brother's wedding behind you. Tell me you're not a little bit wedding-ed out."

She blew out a long, deep breath. "I thought I could keep all these balls in the air at the same time, but, you're right. No more wedding talk for…a few months, anyway."

He kissed her. "Good. Gives me time to plan the perfect surprise proposal." He pretended to frown. "But whatever will we do in the meantime?"

He put one finger in the air as if suddenly being struck by an idea. "We do have my Christmas present upstairs…waiting."

She wrapped her arms around him and hugged him fiercely. "That reminds me. Your real present is at the shop. Let's head down there and I'll call Mom. We'll have breakfast then go to Jack's together."

She laughed at his crestfallen pout. "Don't worry," she promised. "We'll come home early and I'll let you pick one toy to play with."

His grin told her he already knew which he planned to choose. "Boots!" he exclaimed. "Where are my boots?"

Ten minutes later, they trekked through the half inch of new snow that had fallen overnight. There were dog tracks and deer tracks and little prints she couldn't recognize. She'd picked up a strong enough cell signal from the second-floor bedroom to call her mother. Rosaline had sounded thrilled—touched, actually—to be invited for breakfast. She was already up and dressed, as Rachel had expected, so they didn't have much time.

Rufus opened the shop and held the door for her. It was almost as cold inside as out. Almost. Fortunately, the skylights made the interior bright and welcoming. Her gift to him was plainly visible on his workbench.

He removed his gloves. "Should I build a fire, first?"

She shook her head. "No. This won't take long. It isn't a big deal, Rufus. I didn't know what to get you so, like you, I asked someone's advice."

"Who?"

"Open it up. You'll figure it out."

He tore off the shiny red paper to reveal a zippered leather satchel about the size of a woman's medium clutch purse. He examined it with interest then quickly unzipped it. The sound reminded her of undressing him the night before, but she swallowed sharply and focused on the gift.

The front half parted, revealing a set of carving knives with an assortment of blades. They were high end and expensive, although she'd found a great last-minute bargain online.

"I talked to Carl Tanninger a while ago when I sold one of his spears. I asked him what inspired him to do what he did. He said the wood talks to him. That sounded so much like your creative process I thought you might like to try talking back to the wood. Seeing what comes out of the conversation."

He didn't speak right away but when he looked at her,

she could tell he was touched. "This is an amazingly thoughtful gift, Rachel. My fingers are itching to try these. I can feel their energy. You might know me better than I know myself."

She did know him because he let her past the facade—even when he kept the rest of the world at bay. She was too happy to speak, but she managed to squeak out a simple, "Good."

He rezipped the case and set it on the shelf above his workspace. "Soon, my friends," he said, patting it as he did the dogs. "First, we have one more present to give."

Rachel shook her head. "You already gave me mine," she said, touching her beautiful earrings.

"This is something I made." He crooked his finger for her to follow him deeper into his lair—a place he probably counted on her never stepping foot. In the far corner, covered with one of his large, polishing cloths stood a blockish, birdcage-shaped object. Bigger than any of the Dreamhouses he'd made to date.

But when he pulled away the cloth, she saw that's what it was. Or was it? With a click, the two halves opened to form a W. She let out a small gasp. "It's a doll-house," she exclaimed.

The two-story masterpiece was made entirely of carved wood, bark, twigs, pine needles—the flora and fauna of the Black Hills. "Rufus, it's amazing. When did you have time?"

"I made it a long time ago—before the Dreamhouses. It was a hobby. Killing time. Off and on. Mostly in the winter. But as I was working it, I started to see it as a gift I'd want a child to have. My child. And after a few years, the hope that I might meet someone and have a family became more of a dream than a possibility. Until you came into my life."

She hugged him, tears blurring her vision. "It's a wonderful, wonderful gift, Rufus. Thank you."

He gave her a quick kiss, then turned her around to look at it again. "You missed something."

She squatted so she'd have a better view. The detail was impressive. A fireplace made of tiny stones. A wooden cradle in the baby's room. A four-poster bed in the master bedroom. But in the middle of the bed was something that didn't belong. She leaned in closer.

For a second, the reality of what she was seeing didn't register. A diamond winked at her. Without conscious thought, she reached up to make sure her earrings were still in place. Then she looked at Rufus, who was grinning. "Surprise."

She looked back at the two-carat stone in a classic, vintage setting and let out a loud whoop. "What was that about waiting?"

He splayed his hands. "Engaged is not the same as married. We can be engaged for as long as you want…if you promise to marry me someday, Rachel Grey." He went down on one knee. "Will you?"

She couldn't find her voice at first. Her heart was beating too hard. But for once the critical voice in her head was silent. Or maybe the joy she felt simply drowned it out.

She held up the ring, admiring the simple design and patina that came from time and wear. "Your mother's?" she asked.

"And grandmother's before her. Mom changed the setting and you can, too, of course."

She wiggled the ring over her knuckle and held out her hand to make use of a shaft of light coming in through the skylight above them. "It's lovely," she said. "The cut of the diamond matches my earrings. I don't know how you did this—maybe you are part mysterious yeti after all—but…my answer is yes. In the fairly near future. After I catch my breath and we figure out what's happening with your business and mine, I will marry you, Rufus Miller."

His reaction wasn't quite what she was expecting. Instead of happy, excited or thrilled, he looked sheepish.

"What?"

He pretended to loosen his collar. "I suppose I might have picked a better time to tell you this, but… um… my name is Rob Milne. Miller was my great-grandparents' name. The original cabin was known as the Miller place. Rufus was my childhood dog's name. When I moved here, I became Rufus Miller. In New York, you can buy a new identity pretty darn cheap. At the time, I thought it was the only way to leave the R. J. Milne part of me behind. But, legally, my name is Robin James Milne. And that's the name I'd like you to share."

She didn't know whether to laugh or hit him over the head with his dollhouse. She decided to kiss him instead. "Fine. Rob, Robin, Rufus. The name doesn't matter because you're still you. But—" she made a face "—that means I just agreed to marry a man whose name I didn't even know." She paused dramatically. "If you ever tell that to my mother, it'll be grounds for divorce. Agreed?"

He leaned his forehead against hers and said, softly, "Agreed."

"I believe you. Do you know why?" She didn't wait for him to answer. "I believe you because that first day at Char's you dropped off two Dreamhouses. One, I sold. One, I bought."

He made a tsking sound. "You paid full price."

She nodded. "I know. But I had to have it. Because I finally knew exactly what I desired most in the world. When I got back to the cottage, I wrote my wish on a piece of paper and stuffed it down the chimney to wait for my dream to come true. And it worked."

"What did you write?"

She couldn't resist teasing him just a bit. "Something about a guy with three dogs and a thing for sex toys."

He pulled her close and gave her a squeeze. "Tell me."

She closed her eyes and pictured the single word she'd printed in block letters: HIM.

"You're not going to tell me, are you?"

"I can't. It might jinx our future. Do you know for sure what happens if your dream comes true and you blab about it? You don't, do you?"

"No. Not really."

She rose up on her tiptoes to kiss him. "Then, let's not tempt fate." She framed his face with her hands. "But, I can tell you really, really want to know, so I'll make you a deal. We'll open the Dreamhouse on our fiftieth wedding anniversary and read what it says together. Okay?"

The look of love, humor and indulgence in his eyes said it all. But he added for good measure, "Deal."

* * * * *

Kay Young returned to woozy consciousness to find that she was lying on a soft sofa beneath a heap of quilts near a cheerfully burning fire. When she tried to move, however, everything hurt, and she groaned.

At once she heard a sound, then a stranger with a hard, harsh face was squatting beside her. "Shh," he said softly. "You're safe here. I promise."

"I have to go," she said weakly, struggling against pain. "He'll find me. He can't find me."

"Easy, lady," he said quietly. "You're hurt. No one's going to find you here."

"He will," she said desperately, terror clutching at her insides. "He always finds me!"

"Easy," he said again. "There's a blizzard outside. No one's getting here tonight, not even the doctor. I know, because I tried."

"Doctor? I don't need a doctor! I've got to get away."

"There's nowhere to go tonight," he said levelly. "And if I thought you could stand, I'd take you to a window and show you."

But even as she tried once more to pull away the quilts, she remembered something else: this man had been gentle when he'd found her beside the road, even when she had kicked and clawed. He hadn't hurt her.

Terror receded just a bit. She looked at him and detected signs of true concern there.

The terror eased another notch and she let her head sag on the pillow. "He always finds me," she whispered.

"Not here. Not tonight. That much I can guarantee."

Will Kay's mysterious rescuer protect her
from her worst fears?
Find out in HER HERO IN HIDING by
New York Times *bestselling author Rachel Lee.*
Available June 2010, only from
Silhouette® Romantic Suspense.

HARLEQUIN® *Romance*®

GIRLS' *Weekend in* VEGAS

Four friends, four dream weddings!

On a girly weekend in Las Vegas, best friends Alex, Molly,
Serena and Jayne are supposed to just have fun and forget
men, but they end up meeting their perfect matches!
Will the love they find in Vegas stay in Vegas?

Find out in this sassy, fun and wildly romantic miniseries
all about love and friendship!

Saving Cinderella! by MYRNA MACKENZIE
Available June

Vegas Pregnancy Surprise by SHIRLEY JUMP
Available July

Inconveniently Wed! by JACKIE BRAUN
Available August

Wedding Date with the Best Man
by MELISSA MCCLONE
Available September

Silhouette *Desire*

From *USA TODAY* bestselling author

LEANNE BANKS

CEO'S EXPECTANT SECRETARY

Elle Linton is hiding more than just her affair
with her boss Brock Maddox. And she's
terrifed that if their secret turns public her
mother's life may be put at risk. When she
unexpectedly becomes pregnant she's forced
to make a decision. Will she be able to save
her relationship and her mother's life?

Available June
wherever books are sold.

Always Powerful, Passionate and Provocative.

REQUEST YOUR FREE BOOKS!

2 FREE NOVELS PLUS 2 FREE GIFTS!

HARLEQUIN®

Super Romance®

Exciting, emotional, unexpected!

YES! Please send me 2 FREE Harlequin® Superromance® novels and my 2 FREE gifts (gifts are worth about $10). After receiving them, if I don't wish to receive any more books, I can return the shipping statement marked "cancel." If I don't cancel, I will receive 6 brand-new novels every month and be billed just $4.69 per book in the U.S. or $5.24 per book in Canada. That's a saving of at least 15% off the cover price! It's quite a bargain! Shipping and handling is just 50¢ per book.* I understand that accepting the 2 free books and gifts places me under no obligation to buy anything. I can always return a shipment and cancel at any time. Even if I never buy another book from Harlequin, the two free books and gifts are mine to keep forever.

135/336 HDN E5P4

Name _____ (PLEASE PRINT)

Address _____ Apt. #

City _____ State/Prov. _____ Zip/Postal Code

Signature (if under 18, a parent or guardian must sign)

Mail to the **Harlequin Reader Service:**
IN U.S.A.: P.O. Box 1867, Buffalo, NY 14240-1867
IN CANADA: P.O. Box 609, Fort Erie, Ontario L2A 5X3

Not valid for current subscribers to Harlequin Superromance books.

**Are you a current subscriber to Harlequin Superromance books
and want to receive the larger-print edition?
Call 1-800-873-8635 today!**

* Terms and prices subject to change without notice. Prices do not include applicable taxes. N.Y. residents add applicable sales tax. Canadian residents will be charged applicable provincial taxes and GST. Offer not valid in Quebec. This offer is limited to one order per household. All orders subject to approval. Credit or debit balances in a customer's account(s) may be offset by any other outstanding balance owed by or to the customer. Please allow 4 to 6 weeks for delivery. Offer available while quantities last.

Your Privacy: Harlequin Books is committed to protecting your privacy. Our Privacy Policy is available online at www.eHarlequin.com or upon request from the Reader Service. From time to time we make our lists of customers available to reputable third parties who may have a product or service of interest to you. If you would prefer we not share your name and address, please check here. ☐

Help us get it right—We strive for accurate, respectful and relevant communications. To clarify or modify your communication preferences, visit us at www.ReaderService.com/consumerchoice.

HSR10R

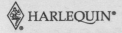
HARLEQUIN®

Showcase

On sale May 11, 2010

Reader favorites from the most talented voices in romance

Save $1.00 on the purchase of 1 or more Harlequin® Showcase books.

SAVE $1.00 on the purchase of 1 or more Harlequin® Showcase books.

Coupon expires Oct 31, 2010. Redeemable at participating retail outlets. Limit one coupon per purchase. Valid in the U.S.A. and Canada only.

52609015

Canadian Retailers: Harlequin Enterprises Limited will pay the face value of this coupon plus 10.25¢ if submitted by customer for this product only. Any other use constitutes fraud. Coupon is nonassignable. Void if taxed, prohibited or restricted by law. Consumer must pay any government taxes. Void if copied. Nielsen Clearing House ("NCH") customers submit coupons and proof of sales to Harlequin Enterprises Limited, P.O. Box 3000, Saint John, NB E2L 4L3, Canada. Non-NCH retailer—for reimbursement submit coupons and proof of sales directly to Harlequin Enterprises Limited, Retail Marketing Department, 225 Duncan Mill Rd., Don Mills, ON M3B 3K9, Canada.

U.S. Retailers: Harlequin Enterprises Limited will pay the face value of this coupon plus 8¢ if submitted by customer for this product only. Any other use constitutes fraud. Coupon is nonassignable. Void if taxed, prohibited or restricted by law. Consumer must pay any government taxes. Void if copied. For reimbursement submit coupons and proof of sales directly to Harlequin Enterprises Limited, P.O. Box 880478, El Paso, TX 88588-0478, U.S.A. Cash value 1/100 cents.

5 65373 00076 2   (8100)0 11651

® and TM are trademarks owned and used by the trademark owner and/or its licensee.
© 2009 Harlequin Enterprises Limited

HSCCOUP0410

HARLEQUIN® *Super Romance*®

COMING NEXT MONTH

Available June 8, 2010

#1638 CAN'T STAND THE HEAT?
Going Back
Margaret Watson

#1639 VEGAS TWO-STEP
Home on the Ranch
Liz Talley

#1640 ALONG CAME A HUSBAND
An Island to Remember
Helen Brenna

#1641 THE ONE THAT GOT AWAY
More than Friends
Jamie Sobrato

#1642 SASHA'S DAD
Single Father
Geri Krotow

#1643 HER MOUNTAIN MAN
Hometown U.S.A.
Cindi Myers